Outlast Your Gods

ELIAS WITHEROW

**THOUGHT
CATALOG**
Books

THOUGHTCATALOG.COM
NEW YORK · LOS ANGELES

THOUGHT CATALOG Books

Copyright © 2020 Elias Witherow. All rights reserved.

Published by Thought Catalog Books, an imprint of the digital magazine Thought Catalog, which is owned and operated by The Thought & Expression Company LLC, an independent media organization based in Brooklyn, New York and Los Angeles, California. For bulk purchasing inquiries, please visit shopcatalog.com/about.

This book was produced by Thought Catalog. Cover by Rebecca C.
Visit us on the web at thoughtcatalog.com and shopcatalog.com.

Made in the USA.

ISBN 978-1-949759-28-0

This book is for Chelsea

I love you endlessly
For your heart
Your beauty
Your compassion
And for helping me become a better person
Baby, you're the greatest

CHAPTER 1

The church felt like a tomb. Not because it held death within its walls, but because the air was thick with the scent of stinking bodies. Rowan scrubbed his nose, trying to get away from the unpleasant odor. He squirmed in his pew, bumping into his father, earning a stern look. Rowan wiped sweat from his forehead and tried to contain his youthful energy. He hated church. Not because he lacked faith, but because it seemed like it went on forever. His blue eyes found the pastor at the head of the sanctuary, arms spread, mouth agape, words tumbling from his lips to fall on muted ears. Everyone looked like they were in a daze, the brutal heat taking its toll on the packed congregation.

Please be almost done, Rowan thought desperately as he tugged at the collar of his green polo. It pulled away from his narrow chest like sticky paper.

"Be still," Rowan's father George murmured, placing a firm hand on his son's leg. Rowan looked to his left and up at his mother Rose, who offered him a complacent smile.

"Almost done," she soothed. "Listen to your father."

George removed his hand, and Rowan let out a long breath, pulling his eyes away from the pastor to sweep over the crowd. The church held two hundred, and it seemed as if it had reached capacity today. Dozens of families sat packed in the aisles, trying their best to ignore the heat and contain the unrest of their children. A couple of babies could be heard wailing as mothers hurriedly tried to shush them.

Rowan sympathized with the babies. They were just doing what everyone else wanted to do.

Cry.

If I die from heatstroke maybe I'll get into heaven automatically, Rowan thought. *You can't go to hell if you die in a church, can you?* After turning the question over in his head, he decided that he must be right.

Bodies shifted in the pews, the wood groaning and echoing up against the high ceiling. The windows lining the church were tall and wide, letting the unforgivable sunlight in. Rowan squinted as someone across from him shifted, the sun blasting him like an ant beneath a magnifying glass.

I'd take the flames of hell over this.

Rowan immediately felt guilty for thinking such forbidden things and he quickly folded his hands across his lap in case his father could read his thoughts.

With nothing left to do but wait, he turned to his favorite past-time when the service dragged on like this. Girl watching.

Keeping his head forward, he swept his eyes left to right, scanning the crowd for young ladies. There. Four rows up in the blue dress. Rowan could only see the back of her head, but she had pretty hair that tumbled down to her shoulders, the color of brown sugar. Rowan wondered what it smelled like and then felt a little creepy as the question blustered through his mind.

He kept his eyes moving and spotted another. She was probably fourteen or fifteen, just a little older than himself. He had seen her before, but it had been a few weeks. She had short blonde hair and dimples that made him feel funny whenever she smiled. She was to his left, across the aisle. She spotted him staring at her and immediately turned her nose up and huffed. Rowan felt his cheeks turn red and stared down at his folded hands.

You're ugly, that's why she doesn't want to look at you.

Rowan felt a little depressed about that and realized he would never get a girl as cute as the blonde with the dimples. It wasn't a matter of effort, but a fact of life. He was ugly, dirt-poor, and lived in a trailer park.

She probably lives up the road in Pine Acres.

Rowan pursed his lips and sighed quietly. He didn't know much about life, but he did know that trailer trash like him would never get a shot at a pretty girl that lived in the rich community just up the way.

They probably hate coming here and being around us, Rowan thought dejectedly. *If there was another church, they'd go to that one I bet. That way they wouldn't have to sit in the same room as me.*

The crowd stirred suddenly and Rowan jerked his head up, a bubble of hope rising in his chest.

Is it over? Please let it be over!

True to his instinct, it seemed as if the pastor was calling for the congregation to rise for the final prayer. Rowan practically leapt to his feet, life suddenly roaring back into his veins. The pastor spread his arms and the crowd bowed their heads. Rowan squeezed his eyes shut so hard he saw stars, relief sweeping through him. When the final "amen" had been issued, the room erupted in commotion as the sweating congregation quickly emptied from the aisles and poured toward the double doors like water in a current. Rowan was about to follow but felt a hand grip his wrist and pull him back to his seat. He looked up at his father George, brow furrowed with confusion.

"Take a minute and ask God to bless your week, Rowan," his father instructed, taking his seat once more.

Rowan looked longingly toward the blue sky beyond the wooden doors in the back but knew he would never see it unless he obeyed. Obediently, he slumped back down and folded his hands, his father and mother mirroring him.

Dear God, Rowan prayed. *Please make me handsome. Amen.*

He opened his eyes again and saw that his parents were still deep in their own heavenly requests. He fought not to groan loudly as he tried to contain his desire to escape. He watched as the congregation continued to flood past him, faces flushed, eyes alight. As he studied them, he spotted another girl that held his attention.

Brenda's here!

At fourteen, Brenda was a year older than him in every way. She had begun to mature in ways that enraptured Rowan, and he stared at her, completely mesmerized, as she walked down the center aisle, ever closer to him. Her dirty blonde hair was slightly curled and framed her pretty face and sparkling blue eyes. She spotted Rowan and smiled, twiddling her fingers at him as she passed.

Rowan turned to butter and the sun melted him in his seat. He smiled back at her, feeling his heart thunder in his chest, his throat tight.

Brenda was the one and only girl in Rowan's life who paid him any attention. Their friendship had blossomed over the past year when her family had moved to Pine Acres and they had begun attending service. Unlike the other girls, she didn't turn her nose up at Rowan's wrinkled clothes or crooked teeth. She was kind in a way that surpassed outward appearances, and her friendship had been the subject of endless boyhood fantasies. But despite her warm demeanor, Rowan knew she outclassed him and dreams of romance remained just that.

But boy did he ever *dream*.

Finally, Rowan's parents finished with their prayers and stood, signaling his release. He kept his eyes on Brenda as he shuffled after his mother out of the pew and down the aisle, joining the torrent of people.

When he finally reached the open air, he felt like he could breathe again. He closed his eyes and stepped into the heat, his skin enveloped by the assault. The sun was a slice of burnt lemon that cast its scalding stare across the modest church, painting the gray stone a sour yellow. The sky itself was pale blue, almost white in the heat, the clouds absent in the burning canvas.

Rowan let his eyes travel across the dispersing crowd and across the cracked asphalt of the parking lot, his heart still hammering in his chest. In the chaos and blinding light, he had lost Brenda.

Please still be here, please still be here, God I'll be good forever if she's still here.

"Hi Rowan!"

Rowan spun on the church steps, almost bowling over a woman in a white floral dress, the familiar voice snatching his attention.

Brenda walked toward him, her face alight in a cheery smile. She was wearing a soft pink dress that reminded Rowan of the cotton candy he always got at the summer fair, and suddenly he was kind of hungry.

"H—h—hi!" Rowan sputtered, caught off-guard. Brenda stopped in front of him, still smiling that pretty, heart-thieving smile, her cheeks pink from the heat.

"Isn't it nice being out of school?" Brenda asked, seemingly oblivious to the tsunami of nerves that Rowan was suddenly overcome with.

Rowan nodded. "Sure is. I hate school."

The smile dropped a little from Brenda's face. "Really? I kind of miss it actually and it's only been a week since summer break started!"

Rowan's face twisted into a broken smile. "O—oh yeah. Me, too. Well. Not history. I'm pretty bad at that. I can never remember all the dates and stuff."

Brenda nodded. "Yeah, that's tough. What subject do you miss the most then?"

Rowan wrestled with an option of lies.

"English."

"Seriously? I would have never guessed," Brenda said, shading her eyes from the sun.

"I like reading," Rowan fumbled. "I already read the one we were assigned over break."

Brenda's eyebrows climbed her face, impressed. "Wow, that was quick! Did you like it? I haven't even started it yet."

Rowan forced his nerves to calm. "It was pretty good. I thought the main character was a little dumb, though."

"Why's that?"

"I don't know," Rowan said, trying desperately to remember a single detail of the book he had just finished yesterday, his mind blanking before the girl of his dreams.

"Was the character mean or something?" Brenda prodded.

Rowan shrugged. "No, nothing like that. I just thought he kind of just went along with whatever he was told. I wanted him to be...cool."

Brenda nodded slowly. "Huh. Well, when I read it I'll let you know if I feel the same way. Sorry you didn't like it that much, though. What's your favorite book?"

Again, Rowan's mind was bombed into the void.

"Uh...jeez. There's so many," he mumbled dumbly. "Probably *Catcher in the Fly.*"

"You mean *Catcher in the Rye?*" Brenda corrected with a small smile.

Rowan felt himself blush and he waved his hand. "Yeah, yeah, that one. It's been a while since I read it."

You haven't even read that book, why would you say that one!? His mind screamed. His defensive voice yelled back almost instantly. *Because isn't that the book all the older kids read?*

"Well, it looks like my parents are ready to go," Brenda said, still smiling. "Are you coming to the town barbeque later this week?"

Rowan's heart soared. "You're going to go to that?!"

Brenda nodded. "Of course! My parents said it'd be fun and a good way to meet some more people. We've been here for a year now, but I don't think they've made many friends yet."

Rowan grinned and jammed a thumb into his chest. "Tell them I'll be their friend. I'll make sure my dad saves some of his famous ribs for them also. For you too if you want! Do you like ribs?"

Brenda bobbed her head enthusiastically. "I love them!"

"Awesome! I didn't think I'd get to see you again until church next week!" Rowan exclaimed and then immediately realized just how forward that had sounded. His face went slack and he suddenly felt panicked. Did she know he liked her? Would she avoid him now? Had he just completely blown it?

But Brenda just smiled that soul stealing smile and giggled. "Why are you so surprised I'm going?"

"I—I'm not, I'm just glad I'll have a friend there!" Rowan backpedaled.

Great. Good job. You called her your friend. Now she thinks that YOU think of her as just a friend and not a potential lover.

His other voice bit back.

As if she'd ever be more than just a friend. The only way you'll ever get to kiss her is in your dreams, dumb-dumb.

Brenda wiped a trickle of sweat from her cheek. "Did you think because my family lives in Pine Acres we wouldn't come?"

Rowan shrugged awkwardly, careful now. "Naw. Well, maybe a little. Most folks who live up the way don't like coming into town for the community events. I mean I get it, don't get me wrong."

Brenda shook her head, grinning. "You're a funny kid, Rowan. Look, I really gotta go, I can hear my mom yelling for me. See you in a couple days!"

And then she surprised him with a hug. It was quick, but it was contact, and that was enough to send Rowan into outer space. He felt her cheek press against his, her chest mashing into his own. He smelled some kind of perfume beneath her sweat, and he wished the moment would last forever.

But she quickly pulled away, twiddled her fingers, and bounded off to rejoin her family. Rowan stared after her, a big goofy grin rising on his face.

Today is a good day.

Rowan stayed where he was for a moment, enjoying the ghost of Brenda's touch as the flock of faithful continued to pour past him toward their cars. He watched the object of his fantasy rejoin her parents and drive away, noting how expensive their family car looked.

"Careful Rowan, your boner is showing."

Rowan snapped out of his trance and turned toward the rough voice to see a pair of boys walking toward him through the crowd. He felt himself tense up as Tyler and Cody approached, his two least favorite humans on the face of the earth. They were about his age and lived in town, the duo seemingly inseparable. Which meant whenever one of them gave him trouble, there was always another to reinforce the teasing. Cody was the meaner of the two, a ragged kid with dark hair and darker eyes. His partner in crime, Tyler, was more slender, but equally obnoxious, his long brown hair the constant source of his attention.

They lumbered up to Rowan and elbowed him roughly in the ribs from either side, their mouths contorted into sneers.

"Don't know why she wastes her time on you," Cody snickered, throwing an arm around Rowan's shoulders. "She's gotta know you don't have the qualities needed to satisfy a gal like that."

Rowan rubbed his ribs and tried to ignore the smell of Cody's armpits. "We were just talking," he said defensively. He tried to pry himself away, but Cody wouldn't budge.

Tyler chuckled and ruffled Rowan's sandy brown hair. "Of course you were. What were you talking about? Which boy she likes more than you?"

Rowan roughly shoved the pair away from himself. "We were talking about books, idiot."

"How sophisticated!" Cody exclaimed, crossing his arms now. "You trying to smart your way into her pants, is that it? Woo her with that rusty brain of yours?"

"We're just friends," Rowan defended, feeling his heart race.

"And you better stay that way," Tyler said, running a hand through his shoulder-length hair. "Because my man Cody here has got plans for that fine piece of sunshine. Don't you, Cody?"

Cody grinned and grabbed his crotch. "Dang right I do." This earned him a disapproving look from a passing woman, her eyebrow cocked at Cody's crude gesture.

"We're in church young man, behave yourself," she said as she walked by.

Cody stuck his tongue out at her back and Tyler laughed, reaching out to grab Rowan by the back of the neck. Rowan winced as Tyler's fingers dug into him, his voice hot in his ear.

"Why don't you just leave Brenda to us, huh? Can you do that, buddy? Cody here hasn't popped his cherry yet and he's looking to change that this summer, if you catch my drift."

Rowan tried to squirm away, throwing an elbow, but Tyler just laughed and held tight. "Where are you going? We need to hear you say you're going to leave Brenda alone, don't we, Cody?"

Cody reached out and lightly tapped Rowan's cheek. "I think he gets it, don't you bud?" Then Cody leaned in, his voice dropping to a whisper. "This summer is all about me and her and I don't need you *distracting* her from the prize bull. You got that?"

Rowan clamped his mouth shut and tried again to wiggle away, but Cody reached out and grabbed Rowan's nipple and twisted it painfully.

"Say yes, piss face. Say it."

Suddenly Cody was roughly jerked away as Rowan's father, George, stepped into view. He dragged Cody away from his son and spun him around.

"Is there a problem here, young man?" George asked sternly.

Cody shook his head and stared up at George, a smile plastered to his face. "No sir, just joking around with Rowan."

Tyler had let go of Rowan's neck and was nodding. "We give each other a hard time, but we're all friends, aren't we, Rowan?"

Rowan's face went beet-red and he stared at his feet, mouth shut.

"Why don't you boys go find your families?" George said, releasing Cody.

Cody smoothed his shirt out, still smiling. "Sure thing. You guys have a great week and we'll see you at the barbeque, OK?"

"Right."

Rowan stood by his father and watched them go, feeling ashamed of himself. His cheeks were burning and he waited for his dad to say something. Instead, it was his mother, Rose, who swept in, ushering them all to the car.

"Come on now, it's too hot to be standing out here," she said, pushing both men toward the parking lot. "Let's go home and get something cold to drink, shall we?"

Rowan trailed them to the family pickup and climbed in. He felt embarrassed and humiliated, hating his father for stepping in. Why didn't he understand that he was just causing more trouble by interfering?

Well, you certainly weren't going to stand up for yourself.

Rowan slid into the middle seat of the truck and stared straight ahead as his parents flanked him on either side. After two tries, George managed to fire up the engine and steer them out onto the main road toward the trailer park.

Rowan kept his eyes on the road as they went, letting his mind release the stain on his day. He focused instead on Brenda and the lasting echo of her hug. Soon he had forgotten all about Cody and Tyler, and he fell into a contented haze.

George took them down the country road, passing through the center of town, lazily rolling past the Applebee's and Walmart, the barber shop and bakery. Rowan let his eyes glaze over the familiar storefronts, barely giving them a second thought as the hardware store, diner, and AutoZone blurred by. He had been to them all a hundred times before, constructs of a world limited by income and opportunity. This was his life, his immediate view of what lay beyond the borders of the trailer park, and they formed the pillars of his understanding. His eyes lingered on the Food Lion as it faded in the rearview, and he realized that he was starving and would kill for some buffalo wings and a Mountain Dew.

"Do we have any Mountain Dew left?" he asked quietly as they left the town behind, the road winding into open country and long stretches of farmland littered with heat-choked crops.

Rose nodded and cranked the window down, letting in a stiff gasp of warm air. "I think there's a couple cans left unless your dad drank 'em all last night."

"We got some," George said, his voice flat. Rowan felt his heart sink into his stomach. He knew that voice all too well. It was the voice his father used when he was angry but didn't know how to express it yet.

"You thirsty, sweetie?" Rose asked quietly, patting her son's leg.

Rowan just nodded, suddenly feeling miserable again. He looked at George from the corner of his eye and saw nothing but jawline.

Great.

The road took them around a wide bend, and familiar patches of trees began to crowd the landscape, filling the dry soil with thirsty roots and reaching branches. Before long, the farmland was swallowed up by forest and after taking a left down a dirt road, the old family truck reached the edge of their trailer park.

Home sweet home, Rowan thought, his mind a swamp. His eyes passed over an old sign that read "Great Oaks Trailer Park," and he silently cursed his existence.

Certainly no Pine Acres that's for sure.

The truck bounced down the single-lane gravel entrance, passing rows and rows of weathered trailers. Residents milled about, either getting back from church themselves or getting a head start on their day drinking. Cigarette smoke and grill fumes wafted in through the open windows and Rowan breathed in the scents of his home turf. Rose waved to a couple of people as they passed, the truck kicking up an apologetic dust trail in their wake. The dust clung to the rows of trailers, adding to the years of grime that clung to their walls. Walking across the road ahead of them was a family of four. They carried fishing poles, and the dad held a twelve-pack of Coors Light tightly in his grip, like it was his oxygen needed to get through the day. The two kids, both girls, bounced after him, chatting excitedly as their mother trailed the pack, a cooler and bottle of sunscreen in hand.

George took a right and drove them to the far corner of the park, across the plot toward their trailer and home. It was a modest thing, the white walls stained and old, the doublewide subject to decades of hard wear. But despite its outward appearance, Rowan felt relief sweep through him as they approached it. He had survived the car ride and that's all that mattered right now.

George parked the truck in front of their trailer and shut the engine off, his eyes lingering on the grill that stood quietly by the front stoop.

Please just stay outside for a while and let me stew in my room alone, Rowan thought as he unbuckled his seat belt and slid out after his mother.

As they exited the car and walked toward the front door, George paused and looked at the trailer next to theirs, a neighboring unit that stood just a couple dozen feet away from their own. An old red Ford was parked next to it, the bed of the pickup filled with old furniture. From inside, voices could be heard conversing.

"Looks like we have neighbors again," George muttered.

Rowan looked longingly at the Ford pickup.

Please be cool.

As if his thoughts were heard, the front door of the trailer opened and a man about George's age came bounding out. He was wearing a cutoff T-shirt, and his arms sported a multitude of twisting tattoos. He turned toward Rowan and his parents, teeth shining behind a friendly smile. His eyes were bright green and his sharp features sported salt and pepper stubble across a prominent jaw. Brushing a strand of jet black hair from his face, the man raised a hand in greeting.

"Hey there neighbor!"

The man's gaze fell over Rowan and his piercing green eyes seemed to sparkle with curiosity.

"My wife and I just got here," the man said walking across the hard packed dirt toward them, hand outstretched now.

"Welcome," George said, taking the man's hand and shaking it firmly. "I'm George and this here is my wife, Rose."

"It's a pleasure," the man said, smiling broadly and shaking Rose's hand next.

"Welcome to Great Oaks," Rose said warmly.

"And what's your name, young man?" the man asked, staring down at Rowan.

Rowan looked up and felt both intimidated and honored that he was being included in this exchange.

"I'm Rowan."

The man reached down and took Rowan's hand in his own. "Good to meet you, Rowan. I'm Sawyer."

Rowan nodded and stared up into the man's friendly face. "Hi, Sawyer."

CHAPTER 2

Rowan sat in his room with the door closed, idly sipping a Mountain Dew. An array of comic books were spread out on the bed before him, but none of them seemed to capture his interest today. He looked at his old Gameboy Color to see if that would entice him on this lazy afternoon but decided he couldn't be bothered. Instead, he sat up on his bed and watched as the neighbors—Sawyer and his wife Gayle who had come outside briefly to introduce herself—continued to take furniture from the red Ford truck to bring inside. They didn't have any kids that Rowan could see, and neither of the newcomers had mentioned having any. This bummed him out a little bit, hoping for a new friend or even a new love interest.

Sighing, Rowan leaned against the wall, his legs splayed out before him on the bed, and stared down at his comics. His mind wandered back to Brenda, and he replayed the hug over and over in his head. Soon he became lost in his thoughts and jumped when his bedroom door opened.

George stood in the doorframe, hands on his hips, taking in the state of his son's room. Rowan sat up a little straighter and waited for his father to say something, trying his best to read his face in the process.

George crossed the room and sat down on the bed next to his son, pushing aside some of the comics so he wouldn't sit on them. As he did so, the mattress creaking beneath his weight, he picked up an issue of Spider-man and flipped through the pages.

"These were always my favorite growing up," he said quietly, finally putting the comic down and turning to Rowan.

"Yeah, I like them a lot. Especially when he fights the Green Goblin. Those are always the best fights," Rowan said.

George nodded. "Right. The fights. I wanted to talk to you about that."

Oh great, here we go.

George sighed and ran a hand down his face. "I don't know what it is with you lately, but that behavior at church this morning just won't stand."

"Dad, nothing happened, they were—" Rowan said defensively, but was cut off as George raised an authoritative finger.

"You embarrassed this family horsing around like that."

Rowan felt like he had been shot in the chest.

"I know Cody and Tyler like to give you a hard time, but you need to do better," George continued. "Everyone was watching and that reflects poorly on this household. Most of them already turn their noses up at us—do you really want to give them another reason?"

"Dad, I tried to—" Rowan attempted once more.

"You need to try harder," George said firmly. "I didn't spend all this time raising you for you to humiliate this family. I need you to grow into your spine and do the right thing, even if that means walking away. You understand?"

Rowan shut his mouth and just nodded, feeling dejected and helpless. A volcano of arguments burned up his throat, but he kept the magma at bay, knowing it'd just end up burning him.

"That's another thing I wanted to talk to you about," George continued, apparently not done with the lecture. "Lately when we're at church you seem disinterested and bored. You seem like you don't care."

"I care," Rowan said quietly.

George clenched his jaw. "You seem more interested in sneaking peeks at girls than listening to what the pastor is saying."

Rowan felt his cheeks turn red. "I was listening. He was talking about how Moses led the slaves out of Egypt. He was talking about how the slaves put their complete trust in Moses and how we need to do that, too. In God, though, not Moses."

George placed a hand on his son's leg. "Look, I was your age at one point. I remember when I started noticing all the pretty girls around me. I do. But when we're at church you need to focus on getting yourself right with God. That's what we're there for. Is that clear?"

As clear as a cloudy day, Dad.

"Yes sir," Rowan said. "Sorry."

George dipped his head, as if accepting his son's apology. "And one other thing."

Good Lord, it just won't end today.

"Yeah Dad?"

George's face softened. "I've seen you talking to that Brenda girl from Pine Acres. She seems like a real nice young lady, but you need to be careful, son."

"Why?" Rowan asked, confused.

George offered his son a sad smile. "She's going to break your heart if you aren't careful."

"Careful about what?"

George gripped his son's leg. "Come on, do the math. Girls like that don't take a shine to men like us. You understand what I'm saying?"

"We're just friends…" Rowan trailed, feeling confused and a little hurt.

George grunted. "I remember when I was *just friends* with a couple rich girls. They're trouble. Trust me on this and save yourself some heartache. If you're going to chase someone, then find a girl who's more appropriate. This may sound blunt, but I'm just looking out for you."

"She's nice, though," Rowan said, staring down at his hands.

Why is he telling me this?

George nodded. "Course she is. They're all nice until they aren't. Then they leave and you get angry. It hurts. It can change a person. I've been there with that type and let me tell you—that ain't *our* type. I'd love a fancy new sports car, but that isn't ever going to happen. You get what I'm saying?"

Yeah Dad. I get it, Rowan thought bitterly, but said nothing. Instead he just nodded and that seemed to satisfy his father.

"Good. I'm glad we talked. Just promise you'll take into account what I've told you."

"I hear you," Rowan said quietly.

"You promise though?"

"Yeah I promise."

"Good. I'm going to throw some dogs on the grill, you want one?"

Rowan shook his head. "I'm not hungry. Thanks."

George shrugged. "Suit yourself." And then he left.

Rowan picked up the half-empty can of Mountain Dew by his side and downed the rest of it. He had a sour taste in his mouth and the sweet bubbles did nothing to wash it away. Outside, a couple birds flew past his window, chirping cheerfully.

"Oh shut up," Rowan stewed, crunching the can in his hand. He looked down at his comics and then swept them up into a neat pile, stacking them on his nightstand. His mind buzzed with what his father had told him, and he felt depressed.

I'm not good enough for Brenda. Great talk.

Rowan could hear George in the kitchen now, taking the hotdogs out to the grill. His stomach grumbled but he refused to ask his dad to make him one. It was his own little protest and he would not cave to the demands of his body.

Bet Brenda would eat a hotdog. Bet she loves them, just like me.

Rowan wandered out of his room and walked through the small living area, past the CRT television and dumpy brown couch, around the kitchen table littered with odd magazines and empty soda cans, and exited the trailer out the side door and into the back.

Rose was sitting in a plastic folding chair, smoking a cigarette and talking on the phone. Rowan shoved his hands into his pockets and leaned against the side of the trailer, watching her. She noticed him and started to say goodbye to her sister on the other end, sensing her son had something on his mind. When she hung up, she stubbed out her cigarette and smiled at Rowan.

"What's got you so gloomy, roomy?" She asked as the tall oaks surrounding the lot swayed gently in the warm wind, filling the air with a low rustle.

Rowan shrugged and kicked at a pebble dramatically.

Rose stuck out her bottom lip at him. "Did Dad have a talk with you?"

Rowan nodded. "I didn't mean to get into trouble earlier. I couldn't help it. Those guys are jerks."

"I know they are," Rose said, plucking another cigarette from her pack. "I've never liked those boys."

"Dad says I embarrassed this family."

"Your father just wants what's best for you, Row," Rose said kindly as she lit her smoke. "He's got a lot of pride and that's his demon to bear, but he loves you and wants to make sure you grow up a good man. You should listen to him. I know he's no wordsmith, believe me, I do, but his heart is in the right place."

"Maybe my heart is in the right place too," Rowan said. "I don't go looking for trouble you know. I wish everyone would just leave me alone."

Rose exhaled a thin plume of smoke. "I know, sweetie. Why don't you go help your dad with the dogs? Maybe that'll make you feel better."

"Am I ugly, mom?" Rowan asked suddenly.

Rose blinked and then laughed. "What? Of course not! You're the most handsome young man in the park. Why on earth would you ask me something like that?"

'Cause Dad thinks I'm a big loser.

"Just wondering," Rowan said, finally pulling his hands out of his pockets. "I think I'm going to take a walk."

Rose examined her son for a moment before nodding. "OK, Row. Want me to tell Dad to save you a hotdog?"

Rowan's stomach growled once more and he hated its insistent wails.

"Yes," he said, gritting his teeth, caving.

So much for the protest.

"OK, have fun on your walk," Rose said, leaning back in her chair to take in the scorching sun. Rowan wandered away from her, shaking his head, offering up a little prayer for his mother.

Don't let her die of sunstroke while I'm gone. Amen.

He didn't have much of a destination in mind as he began to stroll between the trailers, content to let his feet do the thinking. Despite the sun, he felt gloomy and restless. This morning had left him confused and angry, but worst of all, it left him feeling small. It seemed like no matter what, someone had a problem with him.

People are the worst.

He passed trailer after trailer, his eyes drifting over the residents with disinterest. It was Sunday so everyone was outside drinking or grilling or listening to baseball on the radio. Husbands yelled, wives hollered back, and all the kids danced and laughed between the chaos. It wasn't perfect, but everyone seemed content with where they were. Rowan frowned as he watched this, feeling frustrated.

Is this what I'm going to be like when I grow up?

He threaded his way through the far row of trailers toward the woods. Great Oaks Trailer Park was backed by dozens of acres of thick forest, untouched by man or machine. It was the one place Rowan found himself going when he needed some peace and quiet.

Throwing a look over his shoulder, he entered the dense woods, stepping over brambles and underbrush, passing through the threshold of swaying oaks. Summer bugs croaked and squeaked beneath the sparkling sun, the rays filtering through a wash of green overhead. The air smelled of earth and life and tree bark and sap and Rowan breathed it all in with a sense of relief. His shoes crunched over dead twigs and kicked past loose rocks as he made his way deeper and deeper into the trees, leaving his troubles at his back.

He didn't know how long he had been walking when a sudden noise caught his attention. It was off to his right and he stopped in his tracks. He listened and after a moment, the sound came again.

Is that a dog?

Curious, he made his way closer to the noise. It sounded like a dog was fighting with something, the crunch and scrape of underbrush emitting an urgency to its movements. Rowan stepped over a log and around a tree, the grunts and low growls filling the air around him.

He paused at the edge of a small clearing, the source of the noise now in plain sight. It was not one, but two dogs, and they appeared to be fighting with one another. Rowan used a tree to shield himself as he watched, sensing that something was very wrong with what he was seeing.

They were big dogs with short fur, one black, the other a light brown. The black dog was doing most of the snarling as it circled the brown one, its hackles raised, its teeth dripping with thick yellow foam. Rowan had seen this dog before, some months ago, roaming the park, but it was different now.

Instinctively, Rowan knew the dog had turned wild. Its eyes bulged and rolled in their sockets, its lips twisted in a snarl to reveal black gums that seemed infected. One of its hind legs appeared to be injured, like something had bit it, but the wound was crusted and old.

The brown dog had its eyes locked on its mad opponent, clearly afraid, but standing its ground nonetheless. It looked like it had been clawed a few times, the battle in the middle stages.

The black dog crouched low and growled, a deep guttural thing that made the hairs on Rowan's neck stand up. He slunk further behind the tree and watched, heart racing.

The mad dog lunged suddenly, its jaws finding its prey's throat. The brown dog yelped as blood squirted from its fur and it twisted wildly, trying to get away, but the black dog was relentless. It jerked its victim right and then left, its teeth sinking deeper, bringing more blood gushing out of the puncture wounds. The brown dog howled now, its eyes huge, and it sank to the earth, paws scraping frantically.

It's going to die, you have to help it! Rowan thought, panicking. But the black dog's eyes kept him rooted where he stood. They looked ferocious and filled with bloodlust.

The black dog jerked its victim once, then twice more, its sharp teeth ripping the fight out of its dying prey. The brown dog whimpered and its paws slowed, its breathing heavy as blood spread across its matted fur. Its eyes were far away now and its tongue lolled out of its open mouth as it gasped.

The black dog finally released its victim and stood over it. Its snout was soaked and its teeth dripped crimson. Rowan, heart thundering, stepped back and something snapped loudly underfoot.

Immediately, the dog turned to him, sniffing the air. Their eyes locked and Rowan felt terror seize him.

The dog bolted toward him like it had been shot out of a cannon. Rowan cried out and turned on his heel, fear dumping adrenaline into his veins. He ran as fast as he could away from the clearing, his feet thumping loudly, a whimper in his chest. He could hear the black dog quickly gaining and knew there was no way he was going to outrun the thing.

As soon as the thought entered his mind, he tripped and went sprawling, his chin bouncing painfully on the hard ground. His tongue was squashed between his teeth and he tasted blood as stars exploded through his head.

It's coming!

Crying now, Rowan rolled over onto his back just as the black dog lunged. Its body slammed down over Rowan, its jaw snapping for his throat. Its breath was hot on Rowan's face as he frantically grabbed at its throat, holding it at bay for a few precious seconds. The mad dog's lips were pulled back into a snarl, revealing its bloodstained teeth. It snapped and bit at Rowan's face with a horrifying urgency, and it was all Rowan could do to keep it off him.

In an act of desperation, Rowan reached up and grabbed one of the dog's long ears. Gripping it, he yanked it as hard as he could, pulling the animal down off of him. The dog growled furiously and kicked out with its legs, its paws catching Rowan across the chest, its claws tearing at his clothes and cutting into his skin.

Shaking, his senses erupting, Rowan held the dog's ear in a death grip and rolled up on top of the animal, fighting off its slicing claws as best he could. Gasping, heart in his throat, he pinned the animal down, his weight anchoring it to the ground. He released its ear and leaned back quickly as the dog snapped up at him, its body like a current of electricity pulsing through a thick cable of flesh.

As soon as you get up, it's going to kill you.

Rowan, hands shaking, cried out as the dog's front paws caught him across the shoulder, drawing blood. He tried to grab at them, but each time he did, he was struck, drawing more lines of red across his body. He felt his strength beginning to wane the more the animal bucked beneath him and he knew that soon the dog would free itself from under him.

Gasping, his eyes filled with tears, Rowan reached out and found a rock. As he did so, the dog swiped at him once more, its claws slicing across Rowan's face. Rowan screamed and half the world went red.

Without thinking, Rowan blindly brought the rock down as hard as he could, his limbs fueled by fear. The stone connected solidly with the dog's skull and it howled in pain, dazed now. Rowan brought the rock down again and this time he felt something break. The dog's howls were silenced in an instant and its limbs froze in midair.

Panting, vision red, mouth open, Rowan slammed the rock down once more and felt blood splash over his hands. The dog made no sound as its skull caved in.

Shaking, Rowan pulled himself off the animal and wiped his right eye, freeing it of dripping blood. Relief poured over him when he realized his eye hadn't been gouged out, the world swimming back into focus.

He sat on the forest floor and looked at the dead dog. The left part of its head was crushed inward and it reminded Rowan of a broken windshield, except for all the blood and fur. As Rowan stared at it, his heart began to slow and thought began to return. He looked down at his shaking hands and saw they were covered in blood and dirt. His shirt had been torn to shreds, and a dozen oozing red lines covered his chest and shoulders.

He looked back at the dead animal.

I just killed a dog.

As the outcome of his actions rippled through his mind, Rowan drew his legs up to his chin and began to cry. It was soft at first, coming in waves, each sob bringing something horrible up his throat. Tears rolled down his cheeks and he hugged himself, surrounded by trees and silence, alone and bloody.

I just killed a dog.

Rowan bit his lip and wept, his whole body shaking, guilt and terror rolling through him like a storm. He had never been so afraid in his entire life and it left him trembling. Above him, the birds chirped and the sun roasted the world, completely oblivious to the violence that had just transpired.

Rowan stayed where he was, his tears drying, but the shock cemented him where he sat. The sun climbed the sky and then began to dip, the afternoon canopy turning orange and then purple. A soft breeze rustled the trees and the heat ebbed away, giving way to the growing night.

But the dog remained dead.

Rowan couldn't take his eyes off of it. No matter how much time passed, he couldn't free himself from the hammer in his head.

I did that.

Somewhere, a squirrel chittered, as if in response.

It was going to kill me. What else could I have done?

Finally, Rowan became aware of just how long he had been sitting in the same spot. He looked up, his cheeks crusted with dried blood and tears, and saw the black-and-blue sky. His stomach dropped and he wiped his face, forcing some of the shock away. He took one last haunted look at the dog and then climbed to his feet. Blood rushed to his head and for a moment he thought he would pass out, his legs shaking. Once he steadied himself, he wordlessly left the corpse where it lay and headed back toward the trailer park, the evening air cool on his sticky skin.

CHAPTER 3

George and Rose were in the living room watching TV when Rowan wordlessly stumbled into the trailer. He stood helplessly before them and watched their expressions change from bewilderment to worry to shock. Rose was the first one to speak, practically leaping from the couch, eyes wide.

"What on earth happened!?"

It was the obvious question, the one Rowan knew was coming, and yet he could only stand there, hands hanging at his sides, feeling his chest begin to gurgle once more. Rose rushed to him and dropped to her knees, cradling his face in her hands, her eyes examining his tattered shirt and the wounds beneath.

"Rowan, talk to me," Rose said urgently. "What happened? Are you OK?"

Rowan felt a lump form in his throat. "There was a dog," he croaked finally.

George was standing now, arms crossed, looming over Rose and his son. His face was a mix of concern and granite, the two expressions combating for dominance.

"A dog?" he asked. "What dog? Where?"

Rowan pointed behind him, out the door, feeling his chest begin to rattle some. "In the woods. I went for a walk and...and..."

"Your mother has been worried sick about you," George said, his tone flat and unconvinced.

Rowan eyed the TV and knew he was lying.

"Where's this dog now?" George asked finally, his voice hard.

Rowan's eyes began to mist and his voice shook. "It's back there still...I...I hit it with a rock and...and..." he covered his face with his hands and began to cry again, the fear and guilt overwhelming his senses once more.

George uncrossed his arms, his voice like stone. "You killed it?"

Rowan nodded, wiping his eyes. "I'm sorry."

"Why did it attack you, sweetie?" Rose asked gently, shooting George a flustered look.

"S—s—something was wrong with it," Rowan said as his chest hitched. "It was fighting with another dog and then it saw me and...and..."

"Come on," Rose said softly, "it's OK, it's done now, let's get you cleaned up. It looks like it did a number on you."

As she stood and placed a protective hand on her son's shoulder, George crossed his arms again.

"You *killed* the dog?"

"I didn't mean to!" Rowan yelled suddenly, tears running down his cheeks. "It was going to rip my throat out!"

George's expression softened some, but his voice remained hollow. "Go let your mother clean you up. When you're done, there's a hotdog in the fridge for you. Might want to throw it in the microwave first."

"I didn't mean to kill it," Rowan babbled as his mother led him down the hall and into the bathroom. George sat back down on the couch and the images from the TV reflected darkly in his eyes.

In the bathroom, Rose helped Rowan out of his shirt. Once he was out of it, she tossed it into the trash can and began cleaning his cuts. Rowan winced as the disinfectant was applied, hating himself for crying. He stood silently and let his mother work, her hands gentle and loving.

"It's OK, honey," she said quietly, reaching up to wipe at the gash above his eye. "You did what you had to. If the thing was wild, then it needed to be put down. I'm just glad it didn't get you worse than it did."

"Dad's mad at me," Rowan said, staring at himself in the mirror while Rose dabbed his cuts. "He's mad I killed it."

"Don't mind him," Rose said. "He's just grumpy 'cause his team lost today. He's not mad at you, I promise."

"I can't do anything right," Rowan whimpered, cramming his fists into his eyes. "I wish I would just disappear."

"Don't talk such nonsense," Rose said soothingly. "If you disappeared then you'd make me a very sad momma. You don't want that, do you?"

Rowan pulled his hands away from his face and stared at himself in the mirror again. He looked terrible, the gash above his eye curving into his eyebrow. Another half inch and he would have had to wear an eyepatch for the rest of his life.

At least then I could be a pirate and sail away from this crappy place.

When Rose finished, she went into Rowan's room and fetched him a clean shirt. He slid into it, wincing, and stood patiently as Rose applied a Band-Aid over his eyebrow. She stepped back and looked down at him, a ghost of a smile on her lips.

"No one's going to mess with you now," she said. "You look *tough*."

"I look like an idiot," Rowan said miserably. He suddenly felt incredibly thirsty and he met his mom's gaze. "Do we have any more soda?"

She ruffled his hair. "Sure do. Why don't you go get one and come sit down with your dad and I on the couch? *Wheel of Fortune* is about to come on."

Rowan shrugged. "Maybe I'll go outside and sit on the steps for a minute first. I feel like I can't breathe right now."

"OK, hon. Don't go wandering off though, please. I'll heat up your hotdog for you in the meantime."

Rowan looked up at her, suddenly overwhelmed. "Thanks Mom."

Rose leaned down and kissed her son on the head before leaving for the kitchen. Rowan followed her, hoping to snatch a soda from the fridge without another interaction with his dad. As he crossed the living room, George looked up at him, his face all angles and points.

"We're going to go bury that dog tomorrow."

Rowan stared at the floor. "OK, Dad."

George turned back to the TV and Rowan felt like an alien from another planet.

If I'm going to get beamed up, now would be the time.

Instead, he walked into the kitchen and grabbed a soda, taking it with him to the front door and out into the evening air. As the door closed behind him, Rowan felt the knot in his chest loosen some. The sky was the color of plums, the last honey drop of light winking beyond the distant trees. A warm breeze filled the air, cooling Rowan's face as he descended the trio of steps down into the open plot. Fireflies blinked lazily, like some kind of Morse code, filling the night with unspoken beauty. Rowan breathed it all in and then popped the tab on his soda.

"I'd hate to see the other guy."

Rowan turned, almost spitting out his soda in surprise. He wiped his face and looked over to see his new neighbor, Sawyer, sitting on a lawn chair, one leg crossed over the other.

"Want a Pop-Tart?" Sawyer asked, extending a silver package.

Rowan shook his head and swallowed. "No thanks. Mom's making me a hotdog."

The man, Sawyer, shrugged and tore open the wrapper, taking a bite. "Can't stop eating these damn things," he confessed, wiping crumbs off his shirt. "You ever had these fudge ones? Best thing you've ever tasted, swear to god."

"Sometimes Mom puts them in my stocking at Christmas," Rowan said, watching the man. He was still in his cutoff T-shirt and his black hair blew in the wind. Rowan's eyes traveled down the man's muscular arms, studying his tattoos in the dim light.

"Like the ink?" Sawyer asked, noticing. He flexed and then laughed, pointing to the predominant one on his bicep. It was a skull with green eyes, sporting a crown on top of its head. "This is the latest one. What do you think?"

"It's cool," Rowan said. "I don't have any tattoos yet."

"How old are you?" Sawyer asked after taking another massive bite of his Pop-Tart. "Fifteen? Sixteen?"

"Thirteen. My birthday was last month."

"Well happy belated birthday, kid," Sawyer said, smiling. "Thirteen was a good year for me. I'm sure it will be for you, too."

"Don't know about that," Rowan said, wandering a little closer. "Can't seem to do anything right lately."

Sawyer sat up a little in his chair, still munching on his Pop-Tart. "You going to tell me what happened to you? I saw you walk into your trailer a little bit ago. Looked like you wrestled a bear or something."

"It was a dog. A wild one," Rowan said, fiddling with his soda can. "It attacked me out in the woods."

"Damn," Sawyer said after a moment. He looked at Rowan's bandaged face. "I guess that makes you one badass little dude, huh? You take him out?"

Rowan nodded.

Sawyer grinned. "Shit, good for you. You might not like it, but there's only one place for wild animals and that's six feet under. How'd you do it?"

Rowan looked down at his shoes. "With a rock. I wasn't really thinking, it just happened."

"Course you weren't thinking!" Sawyer said, finishing his snack. "Hell, I woulda done the same thing."

"Really?"

"Well sure, what else could you have done?"

"I think my dad is mad I killed it."

Sawyer furrowed his brow. "Why?"

"I don't know. He's been upset with me lately."

Sawyer balled up the Pop-Tart wrapper and tossed it aside, leaning forward. "Listen—Rowan, right? Can I ask you something? Just between you and me?"

Rowan shuffled closer, nodding.

"Is your dad some kind of hard ass?"

Rowan grinned, unable to help himself. He looked over his shoulder and then nodded again. "I guess so. He's always getting on my butt about things. I don't think I'm bad, I just always end up doing stuff that makes him mad."

Sawyer leaned back in his chair, scratching at his short beard, and looked inquisitively at Rowan. "You don't smoke do you?"

"No way."

"You drink?"

"I'm only thirteen!"

"You ever do drugs or get a girl pregnant?"

Rowan blushed at that, but shook his head. "No sir."

Sawyer clapped his hands. "Well, you sound alright to me then. Tell your dad to relax a little." Sawyer then lowered his voice. "Actually, don't do that. I don't want either of us to get into trouble."

Rowan smiled and suddenly found himself in a good mood. "OK, I won't. He'd probably cross his arms and go *excuse me? You mind running that by me again?*"

"Ah, he's probably doing his best," Sawyer said, smiling. "I don't want to shit talk your dad, he seems like an OK guy."

"I just wish he'd lighten up sometimes," Rowan said quietly.

"How long you guys lived here?"

"Like a year, I think."

Sawyer craned his neck back and looked up at the stars. "You like it? We're from out of state, just got here today, like you saw."

Rowan took a swig of soda before answering, smacking his lips as he did so. "It's OK, most of the time. Kind of boring. Kind of depressing."

"*Depressing,* he says," Sawyer chuckled. "Listen Rowan, there's a lot of bad places in the world and this ain't one of 'em. Boring? Yeah, I can see that, especially for a kid your age. You got many friends around here?"

Rowan shook his head, suddenly feeling embarrassed. "Uh, no, not really. People don't really like me very much."

Sawyer frowned. "Why? You seem pretty cool to me."

Rowan grunted, but the comment touched him. *Cool? Me?*

"I don't know why people don't like me," Rowan finally said. "I try to be nice to everyone."

"Well screw 'em," Sawyer said, waving his hand. "Turns out, I don't know anyone here and I am in desperate need of a new friend. What do you say? You wanna be friends?"

Rowan smiled. "OK, that'd be cool."

Sawyer stretched his hand out. "Shake on it, partner."

Rowan took his hand and the deal was made.

"Is your wife inside?" Rowan asked after letting go.

Sawyer's face turned sour. "Ah, yeah. She was feeling tired after the move and decided she wanted to take the night off from cooking." He rolled his eyes dramatically. "So here I am, eating Pop-Tarts for dinner like an asshole."

"I'd eat Pop-Tarts for dinner all the time if I could," Rowan stated.

"Bet you would. Hey, listen, what's this I've been hearing about the community having a barbeque this week?"

"Oh yeah, it's the day after tomorrow!" Rowan said. "You should come, it's really fun. Everyone goes and I bet you could meet some more people, if you wanted."

"I might do just that," Sawyer said, watching as heat lightning began to spark the horizon. The wind picked up some, and gales of dust swirled between them.

"Do you and your wife want to come over for dinner tomorrow night?" Rowan asked suddenly. He didn't know why, but it felt like the right thing to do.

Sawyer looked at him, surprised. Then after a moment, he shrugged. "Sure, if it's alright with your folks. God knows Gayle will be glad not to cook. Lazy bitch…" he trailed off and Rowan guessed he wasn't supposed to have heard that last comment.

"You guys don't have any kids, do you?"

Sawyer snapped his attention back to Rowan. "What? Why you asking me that?"

Rowan felt his stomach turn, suddenly feeling like he had done something wrong.

"I just wanted to know how many plates to put out," Rowan said, biting his lip.

Sawyer softened some, his shoulders drooping. "Naw, we don't have any kids. Just Gayle and I."

In the dim light, Rowan could see something come over Sawyer's face, something dark that made him sorry he had even asked.

Great, now he's not going to want to be friends with you. Good job.

"I—I'm sorry," Rowan sputtered.

Sawyer looked at him and offered a small smile. "You didn't do anything wrong, kid. Just asking questions. That's what kids do. You got any brothers or sisters? Half brothers or sisters?"

"Just me and the parents," Rowan said, feeling relieved.

"You got yourself a girlfriend?"

Rowan balked at that. "No way."

"Why you say it like that?"

Rowan watched as more heat lightning lit the sky. "I told you I don't have many friends."

Sawyer wagged a finger at him. "Ah, but a girlfriend is different. Come on, there's no one?"

Rowan finished his soda and crushed it in his hand. "Well. I guess there is someone."

Sawyer clapped his hands together. "Ha! I knew it! Who is she?"

"Just some girl at church," Rowan said slowly. "But we just talk. It's not like that."

"And why not, pray tell?"

"She lives in Pine Acres," Rowan explained, feeling kind of dumb. "That's where all the rich people around here live. Dad thinks chasing after her would be foolish."

"Your dad and I need to have a talk," Sawyer said, shaking his head. "What's wrong with a rich girl? Hell, they're a lot less work than some of the trailer trash I've been with in my day, I'll tell you that. Course some are straight up hellfire psychos, but with women you really are always rollin' the dice." He looked at Rowan. "Don't tell your mom I said that, I'm sure she's a real nice lady. Don't need her thinking her new neighbor is some kind of misogynist."

Rowan had no idea what that meant, but he gave Sawyer a thumbs-up just in case.

"Look, bottom line is this," Sawyer said, the plastic chair groaning as he shifted. "You want something, you go and take it. Don't let anyone stop you. You like this girl, right? What's her name?"

"Brenda…"

"Brenda, right. You got feelings for this Brenda girl, so just go for it! Don't get lost in your head or let your dad tell you you ain't good enough for her. I just met you today and I can tell you're a pretty solid dude. That's better than I can say for most boys your age."

Rowan felt his spirits lift and found himself smiling. "You think so?"

"Goddamn it, I know so," Sawyer said confidently. "Wouldn't that blow your dad's socks off to find you and Brenda kissing after church?"

Rowan's eyes grew big. "Oh man, he'd kill me."

"But you'd never forget it, would you? I can tell by the way you're smiling that you've thought about it a lot."

"She's just really pretty," Rowan said. "Like, really, really pretty."

"And you're a cool dude, so I say go for it. You're only young once, so enjoy it. Take some chances. Live your life, Rowan, the way you want to." Sawyer paused and then grunted. "I gotta stop talking now before your parents catch wind of this. Again, I don't mean to undermine them, but if I had a son, I'd be telling him the same thing."

Rowan felt warmth spread across his chest, and he turned the crushed soda can over in his hands. "Well, thanks. I'll think about it."

Sawyer sat back in his chair and watched the lightning. "You do that, kid. You do that."

Rowan turned back to his trailer, feeling as if the conversation had reached its end. "I'm going to go back in and eat my hotdog. Thanks for talking with me."

"Anytime," Sawyer said, throwing Rowan a wink. "We're pals now, don't forget."

"I'll see you tomorrow night for dinner?"

"Count on it."

Feeling like a million bucks, Rowan walked back to his trailer and pulled the front door open. Behind him, thunder rumbled in the distance, shaking the far sky.

CHAPTER 4

Rowan was more than a little nervous when he told his parents he had invited the new neighbors over for dinner, but neither George nor Rose seemed bothered. In fact, they responded with enthusiasm and agreed it was a good idea. George had merely grunted and nodded at the news, while Rose smiled and declared it was a fantastic opportunity to get to know them better.

The next day while George was at work, Rowan went with Rose to the supermarket to get the evening's meal. Rowan always liked going to the market, though he wasn't sure why. The store wasn't anything special, but he enjoyed watching the other shoppers, sometimes peeking into baskets to see what other families ate. It was also a chance to get out of Great Oaks for a little while, and that always held some appeal.

The supermarket, a little place called The Farmer's Bucket, was located at the far end of town, past the AutoZone and over by the hardware store. The day was hot but overcast, and as Rose found them a parking space, Rowan watched the bustle of people coming in and out of the grocery. Everyone looked slightly annoyed and he couldn't figure out why. Sure, going to buy food was a chore, but it wasn't one of the bad ones.

When I grow up, I'm going to be the only happy shopper at the supermarket, he thought idly as Rose put the truck in park and shut off the engine. Rowan unbuckled his seatbelt and stepped out into the humid air, following Rose toward the entrance. As they passed through the sliding glass doors, Rowan was hit with a blast of AC from inside. He shivered and wrapped his arms around himself as Rose rattled off the items they needed from the list she had prepared. Rowan, only half-listening, grabbed a rickety shopping cart and began dutifully following his mom down the aisles. One of the cart's wheels bounced loudly as they went, click-clacking across the hard floors.

Who fixes these things? Or do they just throw them away when the wheels break?

"Rowan? Are you listening to me?"

Rowan realized his mother had stopped and was staring expectantly at him.

"Sorry, what did you say?" Rowan asked.

"Can you go pick out a couple steaks while I get the vegetables?"

"We're having steak tonight?" Rowan asked. It was a rare treat, one that didn't come often.

"That's what your father said to get, so that's what we're getting."

"How many?"

"Get four. I'm sure Gayle and I will split one. We'll leave the men to do most of the gorging, I think."

Grinning and feeling excited, Rowan bounded away from the cart toward the meat section. He was already imagining how good that first bite would be when he reached the counter, eyeing the selection with complete concentration. There were dozens of options, all wrapped up and ready to be thrown on the grill. He bit his lip, examining each one with careful focus. If he got bad ones, it could ruin the entire dinner.

Do I get thick or thin ones? Are they better with the bone or without? That one over there looks like it has a lot of fat on it. Is that good?

Fighting off a rising panic attack, Rowan reached down and grabbed four of them, stacking them neatly, one on top of the other. He stared down at his selection and decided that he had made the absolute best choice available. Content, he turned and almost ran into Brenda.

"Whoa, someone's hungry!" Brenda laughed, jumping back.

Rowan went white, completely caught off guard. He gripped the steaks and his mouth fell open, gasping for words. What was *she* doing here!?

"H—hi," Rowan babbled lamely.

"Are you getting stuff for the barbeque tomorrow night?" Brenda asked, looking at the mountain of meat in Rowan's arms.

"N—no, we're having the neighbors over for dinner," Rowan said, struggling inexplicably for breath. "Mom said I should pick out the steaks."

"They look yummy!" Brenda said. She frowned suddenly and pointed to the Band-Aid over Rowan's eyebrow. "What happened to your face?"

Rowan turned red and he quickly shrugged. "Ah nothing. Just cut it while I was out in the woods yesterday. I'm OK."

"You gotta be careful," Brenda lectured kindly. "You need your eyes to pick out all that good steak. You got some big ones there."

Rowan felt a sudden swell of pride. "Yeah, I sometimes grill with my dad so I know what the good ones are."

Liar, liar, butt on fire.

Brenda nodded, impressed. "My dad always burns the food when he grills. I don't think he ever learned how to do it right. Mostly we just order food or go out."

"Have you been to the Applebee's?" Rowan asked, "It's really, really good. Probably my favorite place."

Brenda shook her head. "No, Dad says that's a one-star joint for one-star people."

Rowan blushed again, shame washing over him like an ocean. Brenda saw his reaction and realized what she had said and quickly tried to smooth it over.

"But my dad is dumb and I don't like half the places we go! I bet I'd love Applebee's!"

A new voice came then, from behind Rowan. "Maybe we can go tonight."

Rowan turned and felt his stomach drop. Cody walked toward them, smiling, his hair combed off to the side. Rowan had never seen it like that before and immediately thought it looked stupid.

Cody came to Rowan's side and stared down at the pile of meat in his arms. "Damn, is that all for you? You eat all that and you're going to get fat like your mom!"

Brenda put her hands on her hips and frowned at Cody. "Hey, be nice. If you're not, then I'm not going to go to Applebee's with you."

The world crashed in on itself in waves of chaos and confusion. Rowan looked first to Brenda, and then back at Cody, who stood grinning like the Devil.

What the heck is going on?!

"Did...did you two come to the store together?" Rowan finally asked, his mouth dry.

Cody grinned even harder. "Yep. My mom was talking to Brenda's mom at church yesterday and they decided to go together to get stuff for the barbeque. So I decided to tag along." Cody stepped closer to Rowan. "Me and Brenda have been hanging out *all day*."

"Your mom is really nice," Brenda said, addressing Cody. "Mine's useless when it comes to planning so it's a good thing she has help. Oh, and earlier this morning Cody taught me how to play Xbox. It was really fun!"

"She took a little coaching, but she was getting killstreaks in *Call of Duty* pretty quick after I showed her what to do," Cody gloated.

Rowan wanted to rip his teeth out. He stood frozen in place, each revelation striking his heart like a hammer. His mind was spinning and he felt like he would scream and cry all at once. Cody and Brenda had been together *all day*? Cody was the worst human being on earth, why was Brenda not repulsed by him!?

"You OK, buddy?" Cody asked, mock concern written across his face. "You're looking a little pale."

"I'm fine," Rowan said quietly, not wanting to look at him. His stomach churned and his blood boiled.

This is wrong, this is so, so wrong. Of all people, why him? WHY?

"Our moms are here somewhere," Brenda announced. "We should probably go find them, Cody."

"You lead, I'll follow," Cody said with some bravado. Again, Rowan was overwhelmed with hatred. He wanted to beat him to death with a piece of steak.

"Maybe we can convince them to go to Applebee's for dinner tonight," Brenda giggled, her soft blonde hair rolling across her shoulders as she laughed.

"I'll twist their arm. I'm a pretty convincing guy when I want to be," Cody assured, sliding Rowan a secret look dripping with meaning.

I hope you die of food poisoning, you miserable cow.

Brenda touched Rowan's arm, snapping him from his murderous thoughts.

"I'll see you tomorrow at the barbeque?"

"U—uh, yeah. I'll see you then."

Cody patted Rowan roughly on the back. "I'll be there too! Don't worry, we'll fill you in on all the fun we have tonight."

"I kind of want to play Xbox again," Brenda said as she began to follow Cody.

"Bye…" Rowan whispered, watching them go. His heart felt like it had been destroyed, leaving behind an empty cavity filled with dripping blood. Cody and Brenda disappeared, chatting candidly to one another, and Rowan felt like a ghost.

Why. Why God? Why are you torturing me like this? Rowan thought, a lump in his throat. *Haven't I tried to be good? Why are you punishing me like this?*

"Damn it all," Rowan spat, surprised by his own vulgarity. But it made him feel a little better, the edge of his anger dulled some. He swallowed hard, his brow furrowed.

"Bastard," he ventured, "Stupid, ugly, dumb bastard."

Feeling miserably depressed and wronged, Rowan wandered away from the meat counter to find his mom. When he found her, she noticed his gloomy mood and asked what was wrong. Rowan lied and said he was fine, but his energy was drained, his mind a marsh. He just couldn't believe Brenda would hang out with a jerk like Cody. As they finished shopping, Rowan thought back on what his dad had told him the day before.

Maybe he's right. Maybe I'm just not good enough.

The car ride home was a sullen affair, the air muted between him and Rose. She prodded and pried, trying to understand her son's sudden drop in attitude, and so Rowan finally lied and told her he had a stomachache. It wasn't much of a lie though. He *did* feel like he was going to puke.

Dear God, Rowan prayed as the town rolled past the windows, *please don't let Cody come to the barbeque tomorrow. Please?*

It was late afternoon by the time they got home and Rose once again tried to rouse her son's spirits by keeping him busy. Rowan dutifully obeyed and went to his parents bedroom to retrieve the fold-up card table they'd use for dinner outside. As he dragged it out the front door, he had another revelation that sunk his mood even further.

I have to bury that dog with Dad tonight.

But maybe he wouldn't have to now that Sawyer and Gayle were coming over for supper. He clung to that hope, not sure if he could handle the grim excursion and inevitable talk with his father.

Maybe I'll just lie down in the grave and get it over with.

An hour later, George returned from work, all grunts and nods while Rose asked about his day. He gave Rowan a stifled hello as he passed him by and headed to the bedroom to change and start work on the grill.

Feeling out of place and uncomfortable, Rowan wandered outside to set up the chairs. The sun had begun to dip, spilling a cauldron of orange across the clear sky. Shadows stretched out from the surrounding trees, offering shade and evening cool, dimming the sticky heat that clutched to Rowan's skin.

Just as he finished setting up the chairs, Sawyer and Gayle exited their trailer and began to make their way over. Rowan threw a hand up to them in greeting, plastering a smile to his face.

"Evening Rowan," Sawyer said with a smile, a six-pack of Landshark clutched in one hand.

Gayle, Sawyer's wife, trailed a little behind her husband. She was wearing an old sundress, the same color as her muted red hair. Her eyes seemed distant and hard, complementing the lines around her mouth. Despite the rough edges, her voice was soft and reserved when she addressed Rowan. "I brought some potato salad for us. I hope you're hungry 'cause there's a lot of it."

Rowan despised potato salad, but he smiled and nodded, knowing it was the polite thing to do. "Thanks, you can bring it in to my mom if you want. She's getting everything ready in the kitchen."

Gayle's smile crept up her face. "Wonderful, thank you!" As she went inside, Rowan couldn't help but feel awkward as he watched her go. He couldn't put his finger on it, and so he chose to forget about it instead.

"That silly woman bought a damn bucket of the stuff," Sawyer said, watching as Gayle disappeared inside the trailer. "She knows I hate that crap. I swear she buys it just to spite me."

"I don't like it either," Rowan admitted.

Sawyer chuckled and tapped Rowan on the chest with his knuckles. "I knew I liked you. I mean, who the hell wants to eat potatoes slathered in mayonnaise? Am I crazy?"

"My dad likes it. He always piles it on when we get it."

As if summoned, George stepped out of the trailer carrying a plate of raw steaks. "I like what now?" he asked, pausing.

Rowan pointed to the open door. "Potato salad. You like it, right?"

"I do." George responded and then shifted the plate of meat so that he could shake Sawyer's hand. "How you doing? It's good to see you."

Sawyer pumped George's hand. "You too, neighbor. Thanks for having us." Sawyer lifted the six-pack of Landshark. "Brought some beer over. Wasn't sure what kind you liked."

"That'll do. I got some Coors in the fridge, too."

"Sounds like a plan."

As the two men began to converse, Rowan drifted over to the card table and slumped down into a chair. He watched Sawyer closely, observing how he spoke to George. He seemed so much more formal than the night before, when it had just been the two of them under the stars.

That's 'cause adults have to speak differently to each other.

It was nonsense, but it was a fact that continued to bewilder Rowan the older he grew. It was like once you reached a certain age, you weren't allowed to be silly or crass. Everything was so formal and handshakey and "how you doin'?" or "nice weather we're having." It was like there was this language that only adults used, a careful, tactful flow of conversation that was mandatory during these types of gatherings.

Whatever it was, Rowan found it exceptionally dull.

Gayle and Rose eventually came out, carrying dishes and bowls full of summertime food: three-bean salad, potato salad, macaroni salad, regular salad—enough salad to make Rowan's head spin. He watched as it was placed on the table, the two women chatting in that same weird adult dialect that bewildered him.

If Mom barks out another fake laugh, I'm going to scream, Rowan thought as the four adults joined around the smoking grill. Sawyer popped open a pair of beers and clinked bottles with George before draining half of his. Rowan watched, the air alive with surface-level conversation, and felt like he was sitting on an island, miles away.

Sawyer seemed to notice and snuck Rowan a sly wink.

Rowan grinned.

When George turned back to the grill, Sawyer crossed his eyes and silently opened and closed his mouth like a gasping fish. Rowan's grin broke into a full-faced smile and he felt the storm clouds give way a little. He suddenly felt like he was part of some joke, a joke only he and Sawyer knew about, like this was some big rehearsal neither of them wanted to be at.

With the meat cooked and the beer flowing, the adults gathered around the table next to Rowan and sat down to eat. Before they did so, George said grace and Rowan watched to see if Sawyer would make another face, but he didn't. Instead, he respectfully closed his eyes and waited until the prayer was over.

Rowan dug into the steak placed before him, his appetite coming alive with a vengeance. As he did so, he listened to the ongoing conversation the adults were having.

"This just seemed like a good spot to drop anchor for a while," Gayle was saying as she passed around the potato salad. "We don't have much money, but we make do, and this park caught our eye."

"No one in this park has money, that's why we're all here," Sawyer said a little defensively as he finished his third beer. "Hell, I work just as hard as the next man, like George here, and it ain't our fault the system is rigged—isn't that right, George?"

George grunted and shoveled a slab of dripping steak into his mouth. "God has blessed us with a roof over our heads and food on our plates. Can't ask for much more than that."

"Wouldn't hurt to nudge him now and again though," Sawyer said, popping another beer. "I mean, I'm as grateful as anyone, but I sure as hell wouldn't mind a million bucks. I've been working on cars for the past twenty years and just once I'd love to find a pile of money in the trunk with a bow on it."

"I wouldn't even know what to do with all that money," Rose said as she poured a can of Coors Light into a plastic cup.

"I'd love a big house," Gayle said. "One with lots of windows to let the sun in."

"The hell do we need a big house for?" Sawyer asked. "Don't you like the one I bought you?"

"There's nothing wrong with a trailer, especially the one you just moved into," George intervened. "It's better than most."

"Better than most," Sawyer repeated, nodding. "See Gayle? You should learn to be a little more grateful. Like Rowan here. I bet he wouldn't want a big house now, would you?"

"There's only three of us," Rowan said. "A big house would be weird."

Sawyer grinned. "My man. Keepin' it simple. I like that."

Gayle shrugged, getting defensive herself now. "I was just talking is all. Besides, if we were ever blessed with children, it'd be nice to have space for them to run around."

The table went silent for a moment and Rowan saw Sawyer's knuckles go white as he gripped his fork. His entire face changed in an instant, like someone had slapped him. He slowly swallowed the steak he had been chewing and turned to face Gayle, his voice quiet.

"Really?"

Gayle pursed her lips and her face noticeably paled some, as if she had been caught doing something she shouldn't.

"You got something to say?" Sawyer continued, unflinching.

Rose exchanged a worried look with George before clearing her throat. "George and I stopped at one. Rowan was enough of a blessing for us, isn't that right, George?"

George bounced his eyebrows and tipped his head back, finishing his beer. Sawyer continued to stare at Gayle, his jaw clenched.

"I asked you a question, Gayle."

Gayle's eyes dropped and her face went red, sensing her husband's sudden change in mood. "No honey, I was just talking. Probably had one too many drinks is all. You know how I get."

Rowan shifted in his seat as he watched this, confused. He felt a deep sense of unease ripple through his stomach and the bizarre tension cut into his mind like a razor.

Rose licked her lips nervously, trying to diffuse the situation. "Well, you know, if you guys do have kids then this park is actually a really great place to raise them. Everyone's really friendly and there's plenty of open ground for them to run around."

Sawyer looked at her and offered a tight smile. "Now wouldn't that be nice?"

"Sawyer, please," Gayle said quietly, reaching out to touch her husband's hand.

Sawyer leaned back in his chair and let out a long, blustering breath. "No, no, cat's out of the bag. Might as well spill the beans now that we're on the subject."

George cocked an eyebrow and Rose looked around the table, confused. "What subject? Kids?"

"We can't have 'em," Sawyer said with a smile that was more of a grimace. "Never could." He turned to Gayle. "There, you happy now? Is this what you wanted? To embarrass me in front of these nice people?"

"I didn't mean—" Gayle pleaded, but Sawyer cut her off.

"Oh, stuff it. I can't take your fuckin' mouth right now."

George put his fork down. "Hey now, let's keep it civil here."

"I'm sorry about this," Sawyer said apologetically. "This isn't the kind of thing I'm comfortable talking about and I didn't know Gayle here was going to start yapping about big houses and kids."

"I wasn't thinking—" Gayle whined, but was cut off once more.

"Nothing's ever good enough for you, is it? I work my ass off every day and now I gotta listen to you complain about something I have no control over?"

"I was just making conversation!" Gayle continued.

"We're going to talk about this later, I swear to god we will," Sawyer practically growled, his face taut.

Gayle was about to speak again, but Rowan cut her off, his heart racing, feeling a sense of panic begin to settle around the table.

"Dad, we never buried that dog today."

Everyone went silent and turned to look at Rowan, who wanted to just sink into the ground and disappear. His throat felt tight and his chest was thumping. He didn't know why everyone was getting so hostile and he just wanted it to stop.

George placed his face in his hands and dragged them down the length of it. "The dog. Right. The one you killed."

"I can do it myself tomorrow if you don't want to," Rowan offered quietly.

"I have to work tomorrow," George said, staring across the table at his son. Rowan could tell the argument at the table had soured his mood, the creases around his eyes pulsing with irritation.

"I'll help him with it," Sawyer said suddenly, turning away from Gayle, his anger evaporating in an instant. "I'll make sure it gets done, if that's alright with you."

George looked at Sawyer, almost amused by the offer. "You don't need to trouble yourself. It's Rowan's responsibility."

"I don't mind," Sawyer said. "I don't have to work tomorrow and it'd be good to put my mind to something. What do you say, Rowan? You want to put that dog in the dirt?"

Rowan looked across at his father. "Is that OK?"

George clenched his jaw but nodded. "Fine. But I want you home in time to help your mother get ready for the barbeque. She's got a lot to do and she's going to need you. Is that understood?"

"Yes sir."

George sighed heavily, as if closing the coffin on the subject, and turned to Sawyer. "Can I offer you another beer?"

Sawyer shot Gayle a look. "Sure. I'm suddenly pretty thirsty."

George stood and went inside to retrieve the cans from the fridge, leaving the table at an awkward standstill.

"Thanks Sawyer," Rowan practically whispered.

The lines in Sawyer's face softened some and he nodded to Rowan. "No problem, kid. We'll make quick work of it."

When George came back with the beer, the conversation slowly returned at a cautious pace. The sun continued to sink beyond the surrounding trees and the evening bled into night. Gayle remained upright in her seat and never spoke more than a few words over the next couple of hours, leaving the men to do the heavy lifting. Rose busied herself with the cleanup, and Rowan helped her.

As he did so, he noticed Sawyer watching him closely.

CHAPTER 5

The next day was overcast, the sky a carpet of dull gray fluff. After George left for work, Rowan decided it was time to go bury the dog and get it over with. The whole thing made him feel uneasy and he wanted to put it behind him as soon as possible. He felt like he was returning to a crime scene and he was silently grateful that Sawyer was going to help him instead of his father. It made the whole thing seem less grim, less dreadful.

And yet, as he waved goodbye to Rose and left their trailer, a sinking sensation overwhelmed him.

Sawyer is going to see what you did.

Rowan crunched across the grass, hands in his pockets, as he made his way over to Sawyer's trailer. As he stood before the front door, he suddenly felt a fluttering in his chest, a nervous energy that wouldn't let him go.

Just get through this and then you can go to the barbeque and see Brenda.

Rowan knocked on the door and jumped when it opened almost immediately.

"Hi Rowan," Gayle greeted, her voice thin. "Sawyer will be right out."

Rowan stared up at her, his forehead creasing. Her cheek sported a dark mark, like she had caught a baseball to the face. Gayle turned away, leaving the door open with Rowan standing awkwardly in place, wringing his hands together.

Before Rowan could muse over the strange mark, Sawyer appeared, hustling into a denim jacket and stepping out into the open. He had a shovel in hand and his hair was a dark, greasy streak across his forehead. Heavy bags clung beneath his eyes and his usual spark of energy seemed to be missing.

"Hey kid," Sawyer said, closing the door behind him. "You ready to do this?"

Rowan nodded, but didn't move, his eyes glued to Sawyer's worn face.

Sawyer noticed and produced a half hearted grin. "Jesus, do I look that bad? It was a long night, OK? Cut me a break."

Rowan threw his eyes to the ground. "Sorry."

Sawyer rustled his hair. "Don't sweat it. The lady and I got in a fight last night that just wouldn't end. You'll understand what that's like one day—no way around it."

"Are you guys OK?" Rowan asked, concerned, the image of Gayle's battered face glowing in his head.

Sawyer lifted an eyebrow. "OK? Yeah, of course we're OK. Don't your parents ever fight?"

"Sometimes. But..."

"But what?"

"Nothing."

Sawyer sighed, sounding exhausted. "Come on. Let's get to it."

Together, the two of them marched around the side of the trailer toward the long stretch of woods that sat a dozen-odd yards behind the line of homes. The sky grumbled in the distance and Sawyer lifted his eyes to the heavens.

"It'd be just our luck if it started pouring, now wouldn't it?"

"Yeah. That'd suck."

They were entering the woods, with Rowan stepping ahead to lead, when Sawyer cleared his throat.

"You saw Gayle, didn't you? Her face?"

Rowan stayed ahead of Sawyer, rolling his shoulders. "It's none of my business."

Sawyer reached out and touched Rowan on the back of the neck. "Now hold up partner. I can tell you got something on your mind."

Rowan shrugged again. "It's OK."

Sawyer shifted the shovel in his hands and pinched the bridge of his nose. "Listen Rowan. I don't want you thinkin' poorly of me. I want the air clear between us."

Rowan could feel his heart racing as he met Sawyer's eyes. "Why were you guys fighting so bad last night?"

Sawyer blew out a long breath. "She just knows how to push my buttons. When you're with someone for a long time you learn how to make them tick. And last night, she had me tickin'."

Rowan still felt uneasy. "You were just really mad at dinner."

Sawyer put a hand on Rowan's shoulder. "I know, kid, and I'm sorry if I scared you. I shouldn't have spoken like that, especially when we were having dinner with your folks. That was rude and I'm sorry. You forgive me?"

Rowan felt his chest hitch in surprise. "Yeah. It's OK. Don't worry about it."

"If it upsets you, then I worry," Sawyer continued. "We're friends after all. I don't have a son of my own, but if I did then I'd want to set a good example for him. Last night wasn't that, and I'm sorry."

"It's OK," Rowan said again, feeling almost embarrassed that an adult was apologizing to him.

"And don't worry about Gayle, either," Sawyer said, his voice going neutral.

"OK," Rowan said, unsure how to respond.

Sawyer squatted down in front of Rowan, his face serious. "Look... you know how sometimes your parents discipline you?"

"Sure."

Sawyer nodded. "Well, it's just the same when you're married. Adults don't have parents that'll punish them when they're bad, so it falls on one another to do it. You follow me?"

"I guess so."

"Listen, one day when you're married, your wife is going to do something that you really don't like. It's not a matter of IF, it's a matter of WHEN. And when she does, how else is she going to know not to do it again if you don't discipline her? Her daddy isn't around to swat her on the ass and so it falls on the husband to do so. That's just life, kid. You gotta hold one another accountable. That's how you stay good people. You may not see your dad do it, but I promise you he does. That's why your mom is such a sweet lady."

Rowan stared at Sawyer cautiously. "I don't think he does that…"

Sawyer patted Rowan on the shoulder and stood up. "I'd bet you a pack of Pop-Tarts, kid. It's just the way the world is when you grow up. Now come on, let's get on with it."

Growing up sounds like the worst, Rowan thought as he once again took the lead, headed deeper into the woods.

And then: *Dad doesn't do that to Mom…does he?*

The sky remained a threat as they trudged through the underbrush, the dull buzz of bugs all around them. Rowan's mind echoed with a similar buzz and he swatted at a mosquito, trying to remember exactly where the clearing with the dog was.

After ten minutes, they found it.

The scene remained almost exactly as he had left it. The black dog remained on its side, motionless, and the brown dog it had attacked lay dead a couple dozen yards away, at the other end of the clearing. Sawyer whistled as he observed the battlefield, slinging the shovel down to lean on.

"I'm impressed, Rowan. That's not a small dog. It's the black one, right?"

"That's the one," Rowan answered, not wanting to look at it. The guilt and fear he had experienced two days ago was returning, churning his guts like butter.

Sawyer seemed to notice and he placed a hand on Rowan's shoulder. "Deep breath. This won't take long. We should probably put them both in the ground, don't you think?"

"Yeah."

"OK, then. How about over there by the edge of the clearing? That looks like a decent spot?"

"I guess so."

Sawyer went to the patch of dirt and began slamming the blade of the shovel into the hard earth. Rowan stood with his hands in his pockets, feeling ashamed of himself.

"I should probably do that," Rowan said after a couple minutes. "My dad would be mad if he knew you were doing this instead of me."

Sawyer wiped his forehead clear of sweat. "Well then we won't tell him. I don't mind the work. Why don't you drag the dogs over here so we can just kick them in when I'm done."

Rowan took a deep breath and did as he was told. He approached the one he had attacked and felt his chest begin to tighten. He didn't even want to look at the animal. He didn't want to see what he had done, the damage he had caused. It was just so...still. So lifeless, like a sack of meat left out in the sun to rot.

Standing over it now, Rowan reached down to grab its paws, wincing. As he did so, he realized something that sent his mind into a panic.

"Sawyer! SAWYER!"

Sawyer's head snapped up from his work, eyes alert. He dropped the shovel and rushed over.

"What? What is it?"

Rowan backed away from the black dog, his heart thumping. He felt like he might vomit. His voice came out dry and thin. "I—I think it's still alive."

Sawyer looked down at the animal and then crouched, placing a hand over its blood-crusted body. After a moment, he shut his eyes.

"Ah shit."

Rowan clutched his hands to his chest. "Is it still breathing?"

Sawyer stood slowly. "Yeah. Just barely, but it is. Don't know how. It looks like you wacked the hell out of it. Can't imagine how it's managed to stay alive, but it's breathing. Look at its eye. The one you didn't cave in."

Grimacing, Rowan did and saw that the dog's one remaining eye was fluttering slightly, lost in madness and severe dehydration.

"Oh no...oh no no..." Rowan moaned.

Sawyer quickly stepped toward Rowan, his voice gentle. "Hey, hey, it's OK. It's not a big deal. The thing probably doesn't even know where it is."

"What are we going to do?!" Rowan practically wailed.

Sawyer put his hands on his hips and stared down at the wounded animal. "I'd say we don't really have a choice in the matter. We gotta put this thing down, Rowan. Finish what you started."

Rowan's eyes went wide. "Y—you mean kill it?"

"We can't leave it here like this."

Rowan's stomach rolled.

How did I end up here? Why can't we just go home and pretend this never happened?

Sawyer held the shovel out. "Here. Use this."

Rowan took a step back, his face pale. "I—I can't. I can't, Sawyer."

Sawyer didn't move. "Come on, buddy. You can do this. You got a lot more grit in you than you think. We gotta do the right thing here. That's what it means to be a man—doing the right thing even when it's hard. Even when you don't want to. It'd be worse if we just left it here like this."

I can't I can't I can't I can't I can't I can—

Sawyer placed the shovel in Rowan's hand. "You want me to help you?"

Rowan looked up at him and felt like he was going to cry. "Can you do it? Please?"

Sawyer's voice became gentle. "No, but I can help you. You don't have to be scared. Sometimes life sucks, but you've got to face it head on. Show life you're not afraid. Sometimes you just have to *make things right.*"

Sawyer went behind Rowan and gently placed his hands over Rowan's, their grip one over the shovel. Rowan stared down at the dog and felt his eyes water.

I'm sorry, I'm so sorry. Oh god oh god oh god—

Using Rowan's hands, Sawyer lifted the shovel up over their heads, his voice soft in Rowan's ear.

"Hard as you can now."

Rowan felt a scream crawl up his throat and suddenly his body came alive with a terrified energy. His eyes went wide and tears streaked down his face. Sawyer's rough hands were hot and firm over his own, guiding the shovel's trajectory.

Rowan brought the flat side of the shovel down with all the strength he could muster. It struck the dog's head with a wet, muted clang and Rowan felt something break, the sensation traveling up the length of the shovel. The dog let out a single, gasping whimper and then it breathed no more.

Rowan dropped the shovel and Sawyer let him, stepping back as Rowan covered his face with his hands, cheeks damp, his mouth open.

"It's done, it's all over," Sawyer said, dropping to a knee. "It's OK, kid. It's OK."

Rowan felt like he wanted to tear his skin off, his whole body squirming with the sensation of the shovel striking bone. He felt himself crying and hated himself for it, hated that Sawyer saw this part of him, this terrible, guilty vulnerability.

Without warning, Sawyer reached out and pulled Rowan to him, embracing him in a hug. Rowan froze, but after feeling the older man's arms around him, he softened and let himself sob.

Sawyer stroked his hair, his voice a gentle hum. "It's OK, pal. You did good. I'm proud of you. I'm damn proud of you. You're one tough kid."

Rowan's chest hitched a couple more times and then he pulled away, wiping his eyes. He felt horribly embarrassed and overwhelmingly ashamed of himself. He cleared his throat and searched for something to say, but he felt like there was a dictionary stuck in his windpipe.

"Go sit down," Sawyer instructed, pointing. "I got the rest of this. You did your part."

Rowan nodded and cleared his face. As he went to sit down, he looked over his shoulder at Sawyer and saw that the man had his hand down his pants, like he was fidgeting with something. When Sawyer saw him looking, he quickly stopped and got to work finishing the hole.

It took the better part of an hour for Sawyer to finish burying the two dogs. By the time he finished it was noon and the sun still hadn't shown itself. Despite that, Sawyer was covered in sweat and his skin was coated in a fine brown dust.

Rowan had spent the hour in silence, his knees pulled up to his chest. He wanted to go help his neighbor, but he was worried that if he stood he'd puke. But by the time Sawyer filled the grave, much of the sickness had passed, leaving him feeling hollow and hungry.

With the job completed, Sawyer walked over to him with the shovel held loosely in one hand.

"You want to get a drink and something to eat?" Sawyer asked, wiping his face, leaving streaks between the brown dust.

Rowan nodded and the two of them trudged out of the woods without another word. Sawyer led this time and Rowan was content to follow. He felt small and useless as he marched, trying his best to keep up. He prayed his father wouldn't find out what had happened, but he was fairly confident Sawyer wouldn't speak of it. In fact, Sawyer was the first adult in Rowan's life that seemed to be on his side, other than his mother.

That's only 'cause you haven't screwed things up yet. There's still plenty of time to disappoint him, just like everyone else.

Rowan shoved the thought aside as they breached the woods and reentered the trailer park, the line of small homes fanning out left to right.

"Come on, we'll take my truck," Sawyer said.

"I should tell my mom," Rowan stated, wondering if she'd let him go.

"You don't need to, we'll only be gone a couple minutes," Sawyer assured.

Rowan chewed on his bottom lip, but nodded. Sawyer was right, a couple more minutes away wouldn't make any difference. There was still plenty of time before the barbeque tonight.

They walked around the back of Sawyer's trailer toward his red Ford and Rowan shot a quick look across the yard toward his front door, half-expecting his mother to be standing there waiting for him. When she wasn't, he quickly scurried over to the pickup as Sawyer tossed the shovel into the back bed.

"I'm craving a hotdog and a Slurpee," Sawyer said as he climbed in. "What do you say? That sound good?"

Rowan pulled himself up into the passenger seat and clicked his seatbelt. "That sounds awesome."

"I know you got a thing for hotdogs," Sawyer said, digging into his pocket for his keys.

"I love them," Rowan admitted, but then felt a spike of panic. "I don't have any money with me."

Sawyer grunted. "I'll put it on your tab then. Don't sweat it." Sawyer started the truck, but as he was about to back up, he looked at Rowan. "Hey—breathe, dude. Seriously. Everything's OK. You're like a big knot of nerves. You're OK."

Rowan let his shoulders drop and forced himself to let out a long breath. It blew stale across his lips, like it had been festering inside of him for days.

"That's better," Sawyer said, backing the truck up. "You're going to give yourself a stroke if you keep carrying around all that weight in your head. You got to let it out every once in a while. You need a hobby or something. Do you like fishin'?"

Rowan stared out the window as they began to drive through the trailer park, the road a dusty stretch. "I've been a couple times with my dad. It was fun. I didn't catch anything, though."

"That's 'cause your dad probably doesn't know what bait to use. I'll take you sometime soon and show you how it's done. I promise you'll catch a whopper, trust me."

As they made a right, passing by another stretch of trailers, Rowan turned and looked at Sawyer.

"Thank you. For helping me today."

Sawyer smiled. "You gotta learn not to be so grateful for everything, Rowan. We're pals, it's what pals do for each other. You don't gotta kiss my ass every time I lend you a hand."

Rowan suddenly felt stupid and he quickly looked out the window as they pulled out of the park and onto the main road, headed for town.

"Sorry."

"And you got to stop apologizing for everything. This is what I'm talking about, man. You're wound up like a clock. There is no right or wrong, there's just what you do and what you don't do. You don't have to second-guess everything you say all the time. Just be you and *own* that. You feel me?"

The frown fell from Rowan's face. "Alright."

"But do you *feel* me?"

Rowan smiled a little. "I feel you."

Sawyer grinned. "Damn right you do. See? We'll loosen you up yet."

They pulled into a 7-Eleven a mile down the road and went inside, the promise of food causing Rowan's stomach to rumble. Sawyer got a pair of hotdogs while Rowan filled two Big Gulps full of Coke slushies. Together, they went to the chili machine and doused their dogs in hot cheese and steaming chili.

With the food paid for, they sat in Sawyer's truck and chowed down. Rowan finished his hotdog in under a minute, his appetite roaring. Sawyer wasn't far behind, and together they licked hot cheese from their fingers and relieved their burning mouths with freezing Slurpees.

Sighing happily, Sawyer leaned back in his seat, tossing the empty hotdog box onto the floor.

"I don't care if I won a million bucks and moved to Hollywood, I'd still come here to eat now and again. I mean you just can't beat that shit, can you? What more do you need?"

Rowan placed his hands over his stomach, full to bursting. "Maybe a bigger belt."

Sawyer snorted. "Yeah, might need one of those after a while, but god*damn*. Well what do you say, bud, you ready to head back?"

"We should before my mom gets worried."

"Say no more."

Sawyer burped loudly and then started the truck. Rowan clutched his Slurpee in both hands as they pulled out of the gas station and roared down the road.

For the first time in a long time, he felt at peace.

CHAPTER 6

That afternoon, Rowan helped Rose prepare for the barbeque. When he had returned from his time with Sawyer, she didn't ask many questions, a fact Rowan loved her for. Instead, she had set him to work and soon his father had come home and it was time to go. Just before they left, Rowan changed into a fresh pair of jeans and a new T-shirt after his father had commented on how dirty and ragged he looked.

You were the one who bought me these clothes, sorry if I dared to wear them a little, Rowan thought as he did what he was told.

A short time later he found himself in the family truck, wedged between his father and mother. He held in his lap a massive container of meat, prepared earlier by Rose. The smells that wafted up to him made his stomach rumble, the 7-Eleven hotdog now just a distant memory. Rose carried in her lap an assortment of sides, some leftovers from last night, and a pair of apple pies she had prepared.

George drove them out of the trailer park and down the main road toward town. His aftershave swirled around Rowan's head, mixing with the meat. It was the two scents he always associated with home, for better or worse.

The overcast sky was beginning to give way to evening sunlight, coating the rolling fields in splashes of crystal gold. The warm air hummed through the open windows, whipping Rowan's hair across his forehead, his eyes squinted against the curious sun. The long grass lining the road danced excitedly as cars whizzed by, most of the community pulling out of their respective residences to join in the summer festivities. The far hills were like waves of rolling green, an ocean frozen and carved from silent mountains and timid rises. Dirt roads snaked off the main stretch like dusty veins, worming into the far reaches of the horizon, leading to scattered homes, thriving farmland, and rows upon rows of corn.

Rowan stared out at all this with mild boredom, the beauty lost in familiarity. He wasn't thinking about the fields or the mountains. He wasn't even thinking about the dog he had killed that morning. Like the sun in the sky, only one thing burned in his mind's eye and that was Brenda. He felt a nervous excitement begin to rise in his chest as the long road began to wind closer and closer to town, the outskirts beginning to take shape on the horizon. Fields of grass slowly melted into residential living, old houses and rickety bait shops, auto shops and convenience stores.

The road became more cluttered the closer they got to town, the big church steeple finally coming into view, announcing their imminent arrival. George slowed as more people turned onto the main stretch, pulling them all into town toward the section of road that had been closed off for the event.

"Seems like everyone and their mother came out tonight," George mumbled as he tapped the brakes and waved a car in front of him ahead.

"I think it's nice, everyone getting together like this," Rose said with a smile. "It's good to see people still value community."

"Where are the tables going to be set up?" George asked, flicking on his blinker.

"Over by the church," Rose said. "Along with all the picnic tables. I told Betty you'd help set them up, I hope that's OK."

"That was awfully kind of you," George said. "Volunteering my services like that."

"I knew you'd appreciate it," Rose responded curtly.

George gave a rare smile.

"I don't have to sit with you guys the whole time, do I?" Rowan asked from between them, his eyes already scanning the dozens of cars lining the road for Brenda. He thought he saw Sawyer's red Ford in the mix, but it was gone before he had a chance to confirm.

"Course not," Rose said. "But I want you to come find us as soon as it starts getting dark."

"And try to behave," George added. "I know there's going to be a lot of excitement tonight, but remember that you represent this family."

"OK, Dad."

Rowan felt Rose give his arm a little squeeze.

But have fun, Rowan thought, *don't worry Mom, I will. I got you loud and clear.*

George followed the trail of cars into a marked-off parking area along the side of the road, about a hundred yards from the center of town. He put the truck in park and shut off the engine. Rowan felt like he would explode out of the cab, his body buzzing with energy.

I don't even care if Cody got to hang out with Brenda yesterday, I just want to see her. Who knows, maybe Cody got a cold or something and couldn't come. I hope he's lying in bed right now with a fever and big fat tears rolling down his stupid face.

The thought was so ridiculous that he chuckled to himself, earning a cocked eyebrow from George as they all climbed out of the truck and into the pleasant evening air.

Dozens of people followed suit as they filed out of their vehicles and marched down the side of the road toward the center of town, everyone engaged in cheery conversation, arms burdened with loads of food, and smiles plastered to every face. Kids screamed and whooped and ran between the adults, most of them holding some special toy they had brought from home to keep them entertained while the adults ate and drank and then drank some more.

Rose waved to some familiar faces and George shook a couple hands as they joined the ranks of picknickers.

The line of people filed into town and spread out across the cleared asphalt. Tables were set up, tableclothes unfolded, coolers parked, and the smell of food was everywhere. The sun reflected off the closed storefronts, magnifying the glow of activity. As Rowan walked, he was reminded of an anthill, with everyone scurrying around and swarming the sidewalks and road.

Brenda would be the queen ant, Rowan thought and then felt kind of silly for thinking it. He forgave himself for his good mood and watched as George broke away to help with the setup. Another ant with a job to do.

"You can go play," Rose said, noticing her son's energy. "Go on and have fun. Come find me when you're hungry, I'll have a plate for you."

"Thanks Mom," Rowan grinned. He broke off from her, threading his way through the crowd and across to the church. The street had become packed with people, the long main stretch of town lined with picknickers and screeching children. A couple families had brought their grills from home and were now priming them. Men stood in clusters drinking beer, talking, laughing, while the women mingled and smoked away from their husbands, content to let their kids roam free.

Rowan pushed through the throng, the evening sun nearly blinding him as it reflected off the windows of the hardware store to his right. He squinted and looked for the shadow of the church steeple. When he found it, he swooped low and slid between the crowd like water. He wasn't sure if Brenda was here yet, but the church was as good a place as any to start looking.

He stepped out of the road and up onto the sidewalk, ghosting past more people, and nearly tripping over a little boy who was carrying a watermelon that was almost as big as he was.

Rowan breathed a little easier when he reached the church parking lot. The worst of the crowd was behind him now, down in the street, and he trained his eyes toward the church steps. The big wooden doors were open, letting in the evening air or anyone who wanted a quick chat with God. Two women walked out of the church as he climbed the stairs, and once he had passed them and entered the church, he found himself alone in the sanctuary.

Of course she's not here. That'd be too easy.

Rowan felt a little disappointed and was about to turn back when he heard something from deeper inside. It was coming from the hallway to his right, the one that led into the reception hall that was used for weddings and social events.

Was that Brenda's voice just now? No, it couldn't be.

Rowan trained his ears toward the noise, trying his best to block out the sound of the crowd on the street.

Someone's definitely down there, Rowan deduced as more muffled voices came. Rowan threw a quick look over his shoulder, saw that no one else was coming, and then headed down the hall.

When he reached the reception hall, he frowned. He could still hear voices coming from somewhere close, but he couldn't find the source. He waded past a couple folding tables and chairs, the big room a block of empty space and washed-out windows.

He looked to his right, toward the bathrooms, and his heart stopped.

Brenda. That was *definitely* Brenda's voice. But she sounded...upset. And it was coming from the men's restroom.

Why is she in there? Rowan thought as he approached the swinging door, his heart now sputtering in his chest. He wasn't sure if he was scared or nervous, but as he pressed his ear to the door, he heard other voices mingle with Brenda's. Voices he recognized as well.

Rowan took a deep breath and opened the door. As he stepped into the bathroom, he was met by a scene he didn't understand at first. His ears hadn't deceived him. Brenda was in the bathroom, but she was standing against the far wall facing him, her cheeks flushed, her eyes scared. Standing in front of her were Cody and Tyler.

Tyler had one hand on Brenda's shoulder, keeping her against the wall. Cody was on her other side, standing far too close, his hand flirting with Brenda's shirt. All three of them turned to stare at Rowan as he walked inside.

"Oh great, here comes the party pooper," Tyler moaned.

Cody's eyes flashed when they met Rowan's and his voice was hot. "Get the hell out of here, this isn't your scene asshole."

Rowan stood paralyzed, his gaze locking first on Cody, then Tyler, then over to Brenda's flustered, scared face. He didn't know what was happening, what he had walked in on, but he immediately felt out of place and anxious, his pulse thundering in his ears.

"I said get lost!" Cody yelled, his voice echoing across the plain white walls.

Rowan swallowed hard, but stayed put. "W—what is going on?" he asked, his voice trembling.

"Nothing that concerns you," Tyler sneered, his grip locked on Brenda's shoulder.

Brenda seemed to snap out of some kind of trance and she tried to shake Tyler and Cody away, but they held her in place. Her eyes met Rowan's once more and her voice was thick with fear.

"Rowan, tell them to stop!"

Cody snapped his attention back to her, one hand landing gently on her stomach, the fabric of her shirt wrinkling as he ran his fingers up her chest.

"Shut up," he said dangerously. "You don't get to cock-tease me for an entire day and then play stupid. I mean what kind of person does that?"

Brenda's eyes seared into Cody's, wide and trembling. "What are you talking about!? We were just hanging out! Stop!"

Cody's hand found one of Brenda's breasts and he squeezed it roughly, smiling. "Jesus, you girls are all the same aren't you? When no one's around, you're all smiles and promises, but as soon as you're put on the spot you play innocent. Well that shit doesn't fly with me."

"Doesn't fly at all," Tyler echoed.

Brenda squeezed her eyes shut and Rowan saw she was beginning to cry. As he stood paralyzed watching this, he could feel his blood beginning to boil, a panicked adrenaline rising in his veins.

"Let her go!" Rowan said more confidently than he felt.

Cody turned back to Rowan but kept his hand locked over Brenda's breast. "Why don't you piss off? Just because you're too much of a chicken to make a move doesn't mean I'm going to let you spoil my fun."

"Stop squirming," Tyler growled as he struggled to keep Brenda pinned against the wall. "If you don't let my boy Cody get his taste then it's going to be worse for you in the end, trust me. We're not trying to hurt you. We just want you to pay up. You can't play with his heart like this. It's messed up."

"I know you like me," Cody said into Brenda's ear, his hand now dropping below her waist. He cupped her crotch, his thumb rubbing over Brenda's jeans. "Come on. Why don't you just show it to me. I know you've shown it to a ton of boys before, what's one more?"

"STOP IT!" Rowan yelled, his head on fire. He didn't know what to do, how to make this stop, but he felt like things were reaching a point of no return and it terrified him.

Cody ignored Rowan and continued to massage the front of Brenda's jeans with his thumb. "I'm going to count to three and then I want you to take off your pants. If you let me see it then I'll let you go and we'll call it even, OK?"

"I'm not DOING IT!" Brenda practically shrieked, her face red with terror.

Cody's smile turned to anger, his jaw clenching. "Now listen here you little whore—"

Brenda spit in his face and the room went silent.

Cody blinked once, twice, and then slowly wiped the spittle from his cheek. Tyler stared at his friend, stunned.

Crying, Brenda lunged toward Rowan, but Cody's hand lashed out like a viper. He slapped her hard across the face and she let out a gasp of shock before she sank to her knees, trembling.

"Oh you've done it now," Cody glowered, towering over her. "You've really made a mess of things."

Brenda covered her face with her hands and began to sob openly, the shock of the slap draining all the fight out of her.

Cody began to unbuckle his pants. "Now you're going to have to say you're sorry. And I mean, you're really going to have to *work* for this apology. So pucker up, bitch."

Rowan launched himself at Cody, all rational thought leaving him in an instant. His lungs burned with fire and his head had turned into a war drum. He plowed into Cody with all his might and slammed him down to the floor.

Cody gasped in shock as Rowan rolled on top of him, his breath coming in short, burning tugs.

"RUN, BRENDA!" Rowan howled as he struggled to keep Cody in place as the older boy began to regain his senses.

But Brenda just cried where she sat, tears rolling down her stinging face in a state of shock. Her shoulders shook and her lips trembled, her mind lost.

Suddenly Rowan was soaring through the air as Tyler came into view. He threw Rowan off Cody and Rowan struck the sink hard, his head bouncing against the lip. Stars erupted across his vision like a nail gun had been discharged in his skull. He hit the ground and felt his teeth clink off the hard tile, drawing blood from his lips.

Before he could regain his bearings, Cody was on him, hauling him up, his face a hive of fury.

"I'm going to kill you for that, you little shit!"

Rowan threw his hands up, his vision swimming, in an attempt to ward off whatever was coming. Instead, Cody sunk a knee into Rowan's stomach, sapping the air from his lungs in a rushing heave. Rowan sagged in Cody's grip, but Cody kept him upright.

Rowan's head rocked back as he took a punch to the nose, a stinging blow that was all knuckles and hatred. This time, Cody did let him go and Rowan collapsed onto the floor dazed, his face burning like it was covered in bees.

He got to his knees wheezing, but was kicked back down as Tyler and Cody began to stomp on him.

I'm going to die, Rowan thought from somewhere inside his head, pain raining down on him. *I'm going to die in the church bathroom.*

"What the FUCK is going on here!?"

The blows stopped for a moment as a new voice echoed loudly across the bathroom. Rowan pulled his head out of his arms just enough to look at who had come in.

Sawyer stood at the door frozen, his eyes wide.

Cody and Tyler took a step back from Rowan and stared down the new arrival, unsure what to make of him.

Sawyer looked down at Rowan and then at Brenda, his face incredulous. "Someone better start talkin' *quick*," Sawyer said, his voice low and edged.

Cody looked at Tyler and then shrugged. "This punk was getting funny with Brenda here so we put a beat down on him. There wasn't time to go get any adults, the kid was rabid."

Sawyer looked at Rowan and their eyes met. "Him? Oh I *doubt* that, chief."

Brenda then raised a trembling finger at Cody and Tyler, her voice fragile, her eyes watering. "They...they touched me..."

Sawyer's face went from shock to full dark. His jawline settled and the light drained from his eyes.

"That true?"

Cody snorted. "Please. I wouldn't waste my time on an ugly girl like her."

"Oh you got a mouth on you, boy," Sawyer rumbled. He looked at Rowan who was pulling himself up into a sitting position. "You OK, Row?"

Cody and Tyler looked at each other. "Row? You friends with this loser?"

Sawyer slowly looked back at the pair. "Where the hell do you get off talking like that? You got a lot of confidence for someone who's in a *lot* of trouble. I can tell your daddy never beat you. Either of you."

Cody waved a hand at him, unimpressed. "Whatever. We're glad you came when you did. We'll leave you to sort this out."

Sawyer pointed to Rowan. "I don't think so. You help him up right now."

Tyler grimaced. "Seriously? What is this, kindergarten?"

"Now."

Groaning, Cody and Tyler pulled Rowan to his feet. Rowan wiped a trickle of blood from his lips and waited for the world to stop spinning.

"You alright big guy?" Sawyer asked, still blocking the doorway.

"I'm OK," Rowan croaked. He went to Brenda and knelt down. Their eyes met and then fell away, the shame of the encounter too much to share.

"Can we go now?" Cody asked impatiently. "We're getting kind of hungry."

"I'd advise you to shut your mouth, kid," Sawyer said dangerously, walking through Cody and Tyler to hand Rowan a hankerchief for his bloody lip.

Rowan took it, but handed it to Brenda. She accepted it and wiped her eyes, her shoulders slouched, her cheek still burning red from the slap.

"What do you want to do here?" Sawyer asked, his voice low and intended only for Rowan. "You just say the word, man, and I'll take care of this, I swear to god I will."

Rowan didn't know what Sawyer meant, what he was supposed to say. He just wanted to get out of the bathroom and away from this horrible moment. His head thumped and his nose felt like it was too big for his face.

"Your little boyfriend is fine," Tyler said loudly. "This is so dramatic. We're out of here. Is that alright with you?"

Sawyer held Rowan's eyes. His breath was hot and hurried, his words dangerously quiet.

"I will make this right if you want me to."

Confused, Rowan just shook his head. "I...I just want to get out of here."

Cody opened the bathroom door and threw one last look over his shoulder. His voice came out like poison.

"See dude? He's fine. God, what a *faggot*."

Sawyer stood bolt upright, the tendons on his neck standing out. His eyes went wide and Rowan could hear his jaw pop as he clenched it. He spun around to face Cody and Tyler, who had stopped moving, one hand on the bathroom door, Sawyer's abrupt reaction pinning them in place like deer in headlights.

"*What* did you just call me?" Sawyer said, his voice like crushed gravel.

Cody suddenly looked unsure, his confidence reduced to childish uncertainty. "Nothing dude. Look, we have to go."

"STOP!" Sawyer bellowed, the command cementing Tyler and Cody in place. Sawyer walked closer to them, one hand going to his belt. "I asked you a *fucking* question."

"We didn't say anything," Tyler said in a rush, his face going white. "Seriously, it's cool man. Relax."

Sawyer towered over them, his whole body sparking with violent energy. He slid his belt from its loops.

"What the *fuck* did you just call me?" Sawyer repeated, his voice cracking like glass.

Cody and Tyler stared at the belt, now hanging loosely in Sawyer's hand like a snake ready to strike.

"We're sorry, we were just messing around!" Cody finally pleaded, his tone changing completely.

Rowan watched this with one arm around Brenda. His head hurt terribly and he felt like he was going to throw up. The air seemed so thick and Brenda was so hot against him, pulling him to the ground like an anchor.

Sawyer tightened his grip around the belt. "Say it again. Do it. Say it to my face this time. Come on you *pussy*."

Cody and Tyler shrunk into one another, their eyes like moons, their faces pale as death, their lips locked.

"Sawyer!" Rowan croaked.

Slowly, Sawyer looked over his shoulder. His face was a mask of absolute fury and Rowan barely recognized who he was looking at.

"Can we please just get out of here?" Rowan begged, feeling exhausted, like he was about to cry himself. "Please? I just want to leave."

Sawyer stood where he was like a statue, the leather belt creaking in his grip. And then, finally, he turned back to Cody and Tyler. He took a step toward them and placed his hands on their shoulders, bringing their heads together. He leaned in and whispered something Rowan couldn't hear. All he could see was the reaction on Cody's face. The boy's eyes went wide and his jaw tightened, like his throat was closing up. Fear spiderwebbed across his face as Sawyer finally pulled away and the two boys sprinted out of the bathroom like hell was on their heels.

Sawyer slid his belt back on and then walked over to Rowan, leaving behind some of the rage he had held in his shoulders.

"Let's go," he said, taking Rowan's hand, his voice empty. "You OK, little lady?"

Brenda just nodded and then sank her cheek onto Rowan's shoulder where it stayed.

"It's going to be bad for everyone if you tell your parents about this," Sawyer continued, speaking to Brenda, his voice nothing more than a thin, emotionless rattle. "I think it's best if we just forget what happened here and move on, don't you? Let me worry about those two boys. Can you do that for me? For Rowan?"

Brenda just nodded again, her shame seeping through every movement. Rowan wanted to hug her, tell her he was sorry he couldn't do more, but instead he just followed Sawyer out of the bathroom and out of the church, Brenda's cheek never leaving his shoulder and Sawyer's hand never leaving his own.

The sunlight hit Rowan like a fifty-pound weight, the dying embers of the day spilling over the distant foothills. The heat made his head hurt even more and he shut his eyes against the onslaught, allowing Sawyer to guide him. His teeth ached from where he had struck the tile and he wondered if one of them was loose.

Dad is going to kill me, Rowan suddenly thought, feeling Brenda shift against him. *He'll finish what Cody and Tyler started. I'm a dead man walking. Tally-ho.*

"Where are we going?" Rowan asked, the distant sound of the barbeque buzzing in his head like insects. Sawyer was leading them away from the road, toward the line of parked cars that bordered the road beyond Main Street.

"Going to get you cleaned up some before I take you back to your parents," Sawyer responded without turning. His voice sounded hollow.

"Why?" Rowan asked. "I'm going to get in trouble anyway. You know my dad."

"Maybe I just want to let you both calm down somewhere quiet before you have to start answering questions."

"Oh. Thanks."

Rowan shifted his cheek and whispered down into Brenda's ear. "Is that OK with you?"

Brenda nodded, keeping pace.

"Can I help?" Rowan asked softly.

"You already did," Brenda whispered back.

Content to let it lie, Rowan let Sawyer continue to pull them along, now snaking their way between the parked cars along the grass.

"How'd you know I was in there?" Rowan asked after a minute.

Sawyer answered in that same hollowed-out voice. "Saw you walking up the church steps from the road. Figured I'd come say hi. Lucky I did, I guess."

"Where's Gayle?" Rowan said, wrinkling his forehead.

"Had a fight last night. She uh...decided it was best if she stayed home."

"Oh. I'm sorry."

"Don't be. It's best this way. Come on, my truck's right over there."

True to his word, the red Ford came into view. Sawyer turned and hoisted Rowan and Brenda up into the bed of the truck and then climbed in himself. He sat on the edge, across from them, and watched as Brenda slowly lowered herself to sit against the hard metal, her knees pulled up to her chest. Rowan sat next to her, not sure if he was supposed to put his arm around her or not.

"Your nose is puffy," Sawyer said, jutting his chin. "Looks like they popped you good."

"I'll be OK," Rowan said, touching his face gingerly.

"And what about you little lady? You OK? What's your name?"

"B—brenda."

"Are you OK, Brenda?"

She just nodded, her eyes distant, her cheeks red.

"It's not right what they did to you," Sawyer said, his voice crawling from the pit of his stomach. "I want you to know that. What they did was wrong. A bad thing like that shouldn't happen to a nice girl like you. Boys like that are scum, do you understand me? They're scum. Now I want you to look me in the eye and tell me you're OK. *Really* OK."

Brenda lifted her chin ever so slightly, and her eyes met Sawyer's for the briefest of moments. "I'm OK. Promise." But her voice was frail and the moment the words left her mouth she shrunk back into herself.

Sawyer stared at her and then at Rowan. He said nothing, but he gripped the edge of the truck so hard his knuckles went white. He turned away and looked off into the distance, and Rowan saw something enter his eyes that wasn't there before. A darkness. A hatred. It blossomed across his face like a poisonous flower.

"You don't have to get mad," Rowan offered weakly, wiping a stray bit of blood off his lip. "I've gotten into fights before. I'll live."

"It's not just about the fight," Sawyer practically snarled, his eyes still distant. Something crawled up his throat, but he seemed to swallow it back down at the last second, his teeth clenched.

"Kids like that…" Sawyer hissed, shaking his head, his dark hair matted with sweat. He let the sentence die on his lips and he pulled his hands over his face, his five-o'clock shadow scraping like sandpaper over his rough fingers.

"I want to go back," Brenda said, breaking the silence.

Sawyer nodded. "OK. You got it. But I want you to promise me that this stays between the three of us. What's done is done. We're all going to get in trouble if you tell your parents what happened. Trust me. Can you do that?"

"I don't want to tell anyone," Brenda said quietly, her eyes misting. "And I promise I won't."

"Good girl. You want me to walk you back to your parents? Either of you?"

"No. It's probably better if I go by myself," Rowan said, his stomach dropping. "Dad's going to be furious no matter what. Is my face really bad?"

"It's not great."

"Fuck," Rowan hissed, surprising himself. He looked up at Sawyer, expecting some kind of reprimand, but when none came, he realized he liked the way the word had felt coming out of his mouth. It helped a little.

"You want me to walk you back, Brenda?" Sawyer asked.

"No. I just want to be alone," Brenda said quietly, standing. She climbed over the side of the truck and dropped down into the grass. She looked up at Rowan like she was going to say something, but it remained buried in her throat and she looked away.

And then she was gone, disappearing into the sprawl of cars as the last of the sunlight turned to colored ink, dripping over the fields from the tops of the far mountains.

"She's the one you were talking about, isn't she?" Sawyer asked after a couple minutes. "The one you have a thing for?"

"Yeah, that's her."

"And those little shits…" Sawyer gritted his teeth again, staring off at where Brenda had vanished. "I swear to god, Rowan, kids like that grow up rotten. Nothing good can come of it. If they're pulling shit like this when they're teenagers…"

Rowan stared at his feet. "I know. I hate them. I hate them *so much*. I wish they were dead."

Sawyer, his mood blackened, turned back to Rowan. "Come on, kid. Let's head back. I need to find a drink."

Rowan swung his leg over the side, but paused, the evening wind drying the last of the blood on his lip. "Hey, Sawyer?"

Sawyer looked at him from across the truck, his face like granite. "Yeah?"

"Thanks for saving me. They would have killed me if you hadn't come."

Sawyer ground his teeth together, that darkness still lingering in his eyes. "Anytime, kid. I got you."

Rowan felt something soften inside his chest and tears suddenly welled in his eyes.

"I wish you were my dad."

Sawyer said nothing in response as he climbed out of the truck, but Rowan saw some of the darkness leave the man's eyes.

And then it returned, worse than ever.

CHAPTER 7

Rowan walked slowly back to Main Street, dreading every step. He felt defeated in every way. His shoulders slumped, his face hurt, and his chest vibrated with anxiety. The closer he got to the crowds, the slower he walked. He knew a confrontation with his parents was inevitable, and he was in no rush to get to it.

It's not fair, Rowan thought as his feet met asphalt. *Why am I the one getting in trouble here? Why am I going to get yelled at? What about Cody and Tyler? Why doesn't someone do something about them? Where are their parents in all this?*

Rowan passed a couple tables, each one filled with townsfolk, all happily chowing down their meals without a care in the world. A young boy at the table spat a watermelon seed at his sister and earned himself a slap on the back of the head. But no one looked up as Rowan passed.

I might as well be a ghost that haunts my parents' existence.

The air smelled of charcoal and grilled meats, but Rowan had lost his appetite. He just wanted to go home, pull his clothes off, and die in bed. He gingerly touched his face and winced as his fingers made contact with his swollen nose.

I probably look like Squidward right now. Except even uglier.

Depression settled around his mind and he suddenly felt like crying again. He replayed the scene in his head over and over again as he walked, Brenda's shocked, fearful face blazing in his mind's eye.

How could they do that to her? How could they hurt someone as nice as her? Why would they do that? Why are people so terrible!?

Rowan curled his fists and gritted his teeth. The world wasn't fair and he loathed it for the fact.

When he finally reached Rose, he was in a terrible mood. He slumped down in a chair next to her and when she turned to greet him, her face grew tight and her eyes widened. Thankfully, George was nowhere to be seen and Rowan prayed he'd just stay away.

"What on Earth, Rowan?" Rose hissed, looking around, keeping her voice low. "What happened to you?"

"I don't want to talk about it," Rowan said sullenly, crossing his arms. He stared straight ahead and watched a mother draw chalk figures on the sidewalk with her three kids.

Rose set her plate down and turned away from the conversation she was having with the woman next to her.

"Oh Row, when your father—"

"Dad can go to hell for all I care," Rowan muttered.

Rose inhaled sharply. "Stop that. Don't talk about your father that way. You're a mess, are you OK? Let me get you some ice for your nose. Good Lord, Row, what happened!?"

"I'm fine, I just want to go home."

"I'm getting you some ice."

Rowan sunk further into his chair, a storm cloud hovering over his head. He let his eyes wander the crowd and he spotted Sawyer, beer in hand. He didn't look at Rowan, instead draining his bottle only to search for another one. There was something about the way he was walking, the way his body lurched about, that sent warning flares through Rowan's mind.

He's mad. He's super, super mad.

Rowan had seen it before, that quiet, furious ocean just beneath the surface. It was something his father specialized in.

Sawyer snatched two more beers from a cooler and then disappeared back into the crowd, leaving Rowan to sulk in solitude.

Rose returned with some ice in a plastic bag and Rowan moodily snatched it from her before pressing it to his face.

"It'll help the swelling, sweetie," Rose said quietly, on the lookout for George.

"I don't care about the swelling," Rowan spat. "I just want to go home and never speak to anyone ever again. I hate everyone and my head hurts. Can we please just leave?"

Rose frowned and then squeezed her son's arm gently. "In a little bit. I promise. Just keep the ice on. Can I get you something to eat?"

"Can I eat a bullet? Do you have one of those?"

Rose frowned some more. "OK, Rowan. I get it."

It wasn't long before George came lumbering over, parting the crowd like Moses and the Red Sea. Or at least, that's how it looked to Rowan as the waves of people moved aside as the big man came into view. He was smiling and looked to be in a good mood, but that instantly vanished the second he laid eyes on Rowan.

He stood in front of Rose and Rowan as if trying to solve a riddle, one hand clutching a paper plate stacked with food. He slowly set it down on the table and opened his mouth, eyes roaming Rowan's face, as if searching for an answer. After a second, he closed his mouth, and his jawline ermerged.

"We'll talk about this later," George said quietly, his voice like a knife. "Rowan, go wait in the car where no one can see you. Now."

Rose looked up at her husband, her eyes pleading. "George—"

"Not now, Rose. We will have a discussion when we have some privacy, but *not now*."

Rowan knew his father's reaction was inevitable, and yet it still evoked a reaction in him. Instead of the usual fear and shame though, he felt angry. He felt cheated. Why wasn't he given an ounce of concern? Why was it *always* about how people viewed him? Why was it *always* about keeping up appearances?

What about me? Rowan thought venomously. *What about the bruises on my face? What about my swollen nose? What about your SON!?*

"Go Rowan. Now," George instructed with an outstretched finger.

Rowan stood up and threw the ice baggy down onto the ground. Hard. It burst open and water splashed onto George's jeans.

George curled his hands into fists and he quickly looked around at the surrounding crowd before answering in a voice that was all fire and brimstone.

"You have five seconds before I—"

"I'm going," Rowan snarled, his body buzzing with fury. "Don't worry, I'll keep out of sight. Wouldn't want people to think you were a shitty parent."

And then Rowan stormed off, knowing he had just signed his death warrant. But he didn't care. Nothing mattered in that moment, nothing existed except for the warring rage he felt coursing through his veins.

He thundered back to the family truck, staring death at anyone that looked at him. When he got to the truck, he yanked the door open and then slammed it as hard as he could after he climbed inside. He sat in silence, ears thrumming, his fists curled.

"This is such *shit*," he growled.

He could practically feel the steam pouring out of his ears as he stewed. He wanted to lash out, punch something, break something, scream until his throat tore open. Instead, he sat in silence, his whole body quivering with righteous anger. He stared past the windshield and out into the dimming world. If he had to guess, it was probably the last sunset he'd see before his imminent death at the hands of his father.

His mind continued to boil as time ticked away, marked by the rising moon and growing shadows. After two hours he began to see families return to their cars, carrying empty coolers and sleeping children in their arms. He felt like he had been sitting in the cab for a lifetime before he saw his parents among the trickling crowds. As impatient as he felt, upon sighting them, he realized he wasn't ready for the inevitable confrontation. Much of his anger had ebbed away in the growing night, replaced by a heavy fatigue.

Rowan winced as George came around the side and threw the empty coolers into the bed of the truck.

Yep, he's still mad. Great.

Rose opened the door cautiously and climbed up next to her son, waving her last goodbyes to the dispersing throng. She looked at Rowan and gave him an unreadable, emotionless smile.

Well, Mom's checked out. Expect no help from her tonight, buckaroo.

George jerked open his door and climbed in, not looking at Rowan. He cleared his throat and spat onto the ground before leaning back inside to slam his door. He fired up the engine and put the truck into gear.

Rowan stared straight ahead, his lips locked tight, his fists resting on his thighs. As tired as he was, he began to feel some of his anger returning.

Silent treatment until we get home. Wonderful. Let me simmer in my imagination for a couple more minutes, like I haven't already had hours to do that.

Rose rolled down her window as they pulled out onto the road, following the long trail of cars in front of them. Crickets chirped their familiar tune in the warm night air, joined in part by a chorus of echoing frogs and rustling wind. Fireflies fanned out on both sides of the road, filling the dark fields like stars across the universe.

Rowan could have counted each breath he took on the drive home because of how miserably aware he was of each one of them. When Great Oaks finally came into view, he felt sick to his stomach. As they bounced off the main road and into the park, he tried to enjoy the last view of the sky.

George steered them toward the back of the park and then pulled into their lot. Rowan mused that their trailer, his home, had never looked more like a coffin.

The three of them climbed out of the truck in silence and walked to the front door. Rowan looked across the lawn and saw the red Ford parked in front of Sawyer's trailer. From inside, voices could be heard as shadows bounced across the drawn curtains. Loud voices. Yelling. As George unlocked their front door, a crash was heard from Sawyer's trailer, like breaking glass. Rose shot a look over her shoulder and then ushered Rowan inside, behind his father.

"Go to your room," George said darkly as he turned on the lights to the living room. "We have to talk."

Silently, Rowan obeyed.

Let's just get this over with.

Entering his room felt like entering a crypt. The air tasted stale and the walls seemed closer, tighter. He looked out the window as he crawled onto his bed and spotted the lit-up windows in Sawyer's trailer. Muted voices could still be heard yelling, even from this distance, and Rowan turned miserably around to sit against the wall, with his legs hanging over the side of his bed.

Everyone is angry tonight. Absolutely everyone.

After a couple cancerous minutes, George finally walked in, shutting the door behind him.

Never a good sign, Rowan thought as he scooted over so his dad could sit down. But George remained where he was, in front of the door, arms crossed. Swallowing hard, Rowan stared at his feet, all too aware of his swollen nose.

"What the hell is going on with you, Rowan?" George asked after a moment. His voice was flat and raw, his face creased with disapproval.

Rowan said nothing, knowing it wasn't time to go on the defensive yet. Not until he had taken a couple more offensive blows.

George shook his head, his eyes dark. "Do we have a problem? Look at me, son. Do we have *a problem*?"

"Aren't you even going to ask me what happened?" Rowan asked quietly.

"I don't need to!" George yelled. "I can SEE what happened!"

Rowan shrugged, feeling the wick on his temper shorten suddenly. "Well then I guess you know it wasn't my fault and I'm not the one you should be yelling at."

George suddenly slammed his fist into the wall hard enough to shake the nightstand.

"You do NOT speak to your father like that, do you understand?!"

Rowan shrunk a little, his anger replaced immediately by caution. *Wrong move. Super wrong move.*

George fought to compose himself some but seemed to be losing. "I swear it's one thing after another with you these days. Fights, dogs, girls, what's next? Huh? What's next? What are you going to do NEXT!? How many times are you going to embarrass this family, Rowan? Why is it SO HARD for you to just behave and stay out of trouble?!"

"I don't go looking for trouble!" Rowan exclaimed, breaking some. He felt frustration and fear bubbling up in his chest, a horrible pressure rising with it.

"And yet here you are!" George yelled. "You look like you got hit by a car! What are people supposed to think when they look at you? You think people are going to respect you? This family? You think people aren't going to TALK? What do you think people will say about you? About me and your mother? Well!?"

"I don't care what people think!" Rowan cried, sitting up now. "I just want everyone to LEAVE ME ALONE!"

George stepped forward and raised a menacing finger, his face all wrinkles and red lines. "Do NOT raise your voice at me young man or I swear to god I will *silence* you."

"I'm not a bad PERSON!" Rowan yelled as his emotions began to peak. He could feel tears of anger and frustration beginning to form and he hated that he couldn't stop them.

"You are *right* at the crossroads," George hissed. "And I have no idea which way you're going to turn. I have tried and tried and TRIED to raise you right. I've taken you to church, I have shown you the path, I have taught you to treat others well, and yet here you sit with blood on your clothes and a bad attitude. Where did I go wrong, Rowan? You tell me. Where did I go wrong?"

"YOU DON'T GIVE A SHIT ABOUT ME!" Rowan roared as tears erupted from his eyes.

The slap came without warning and it knocked Rowan to the floor.

"You do *not* use profanity in this house," George panted, standing over him. "Don't think I've forgotten about your little outburst earlier either. I don't know where you learned to speak like that, but it makes me sick to know my own son talks like that. Words like that make a man *cheap*. They make him easy. They make a man *stupid*. Is that what you are? Are you stupid? Am I raising a stupid son?"

Rowan cried where he lay, the shock from the slap ringing in his ears. His mind felt hollow and the world seemed to be spinning, sucked down into some dark, unknown vortex. Tears ran over the bridge of his swollen nose and his body shook as he lay helpless across the floor.

His dad had never slapped him before. And yet it had come so swiftly and without thought, as if it had been there for years, lurking, held feverishly at bay by some desperate padlock of social pressure.

But now that it had happened, it felt as if something else was there now, something huge and horned, something ugly and scary, something that would forever shape the way he thought about his father.

And that made Rowan sick to his stomach and broke whatever was left of his exhausted heart.

George ran his hands through his hair and sighed, frustrated. He looked down at his crying son, his face reforming.

"Get up. Stop that. I'm raising a son, not a weepy-eyed little girl. Come on. On your feet." He pulled Rowan up and sat him down on the bed.

Rowan wiped his eyes with the back of his hands, but he couldn't look at his father. He didn't want to. He felt betrayed and hurt. He felt like he was going to vomit. He felt terrified and angry and sad and horribly alone and it was all crammed up into this pulsing black ball and it was choking him and suffocating him and—

Rowan closed his eyes and tried to breathe. Inhale. Exhale.

Just survive this moment.

He felt like the world was out to get him and there was just no escaping it.

George seemed to realize what he had done and his tone softened. He forced a breath down his throat and then sat down next to his son.

"I know you think I'm hard on you. I know you're angry at me, but I hope that one day you'll look back on all this and understand." George paused and ran a hand down his face, exhaling. "It's not easy being a parent, Rowan. Lord knows it ain't. You just hope you're doing a better job than your own parents."

Rowan said nothing, his father's words lost in some miserable haze.

But George continued, his voice ponderous and deliberate. "It's so important to be respected, Rowan. If people respect you then you can become a positive force in the world, like we're intended to be. I know you never knew your grandparents, that they died before you were born, but even if they were alive I'd never let them near you."

Through the haze, Rowan's mind clung to this odd declaration, the pain pulsing.

George looked down at his hands. "My parents, your grandparents, were terrible people. They were lazy, they were uninspired, and they were the laughing stock of the town I grew up in. If they weren't high then they were drunk or trying to get there. They stole, lied, and cheated anyone who was stupid enough to trust them."

George's hands curled into fists. "Like you, I was an only child and they were terrible to me in the sense that I might as well have been a ghost. The only thing they cared about was their next fix and their next government check. It was a world I wouldn't wish on anyone. But I got through it and I swore to myself that I would never, ever live a life of shame like they did. Because I saw what it did to a person. How it changed them. How it changed me. I barely even recognize the kid that crawled out of that hole."

George was silent for a moment and then blinked, as if coming out of deep trance. "Look, the reason I'm telling you this is so that you'll understand my motives. I've been on the other side of shame. I've been disrespected because of who I was and what family I was a part of. If I seem hard on you then it's because I'm afraid that I'm failing you in some way. That I'm allowing you to grow into a life of morale neglect. So you tell me—am I failing you, Rowan? Is there something I can do to stop all this dangerous behavior?"

Rowan didn't know what to say, how to respond to this awkward revelation, this unfurling of his father that he had never been exposed to before. Rowan shut his eyes before they could spill more sorrow.

Just love me.

But Rowan couldn't say that. Not now with his cheek still smarting and his head still ringing. Right now he didn't want that. He didn't want anything to do with his father. He didn't care about what had happened to him in the past. He didn't care about his grand-parents and their terrible life. All he wanted was what everyone else seemed to have.

Just be my dad.

And then a thought struck him that was so sad that he started to cry again.

Maybe it's too late.

George sat and watched Rowan cry, saying nothing. No hand on the shoulder, no words of comfort, no apology. When Rowan got him-self under control, George cleared his throat, as if his silence had been an allowance in some way.

"Just get it together, Rowan. That's all I'm asking. No more fights. No more bloody lips. Do you understand? This behavior has to end. From now on you stay out of trouble and keep your nose clean. Nothing good will come of it if you continue on like this. Trust me. One day you'll thank me."

I doubt it.

The anger was coming back.

Then the pat on the leg came, the period at the end of the sen-tence, the door closing on the conversation.

George stood and walked to the door, opening it. He turned around, his voice back to neutral.

"Why don't you get some sleep? It's been a long day."

Rowan scrubbed a tear from his eye, hating it. "OK, Dad."

"Goodnight, son."

Fuck you.

"Night, Dad."

And then the door closed and Rowan could just picture his father mentally ticking off a box in his head.

Spoke with son about bad behavior. I did my part, the rest is in God's hands.

Rowan looked up at the ceiling and gave it the middle finger, teeth clenched, his eyes threatening another outburst of tears.

Chest heaving, Rowan crawled over to the window by his head-board and looked out, scrubbing his eyes as he did so.

Stop crying. Don't give him that, he thought angrily as he slid the Plexiglass panel open to let in the night air. He propped his chin up on the sill and stared out at the glowing darkness. The park was alive with light, little pockets of warmth that pushed away the wall of black. From his window, Rowan had a direct line of sight straight to Sawyer's trailer. He stared at it, wondering if his friend's night was going as badly as his own. The wind felt good and it cooled his burning face a bit, blowing some of his temper away.

I'll never be good enough for Dad, Rowan thought as he watched Sawyer's blinds for shadows. *No matter what I do, I'll always be a disappointment.*

Rowan rubbed his cheek and tried to fight his surging emotions. He focused on the wind and how it blustered through the window and around his room. How it seemed to whisper to him.

It's over. At least, if nothing else, it's over. For now.

He didn't know how long he had been sitting there when suddenly Sawyer's front door burst open, spilling light out onto the dusty earth. Sawyer stumbled down the steps, slamming the door shut behind him hard. Rowan sat up a little straighter, his mind pulled from the depths of his thoughts.

Sawyer was shirtless and he carried a bottle in one hand. He appeared to be drunk and was muttering angrily to himself. He stood on the front lawn and took a long pull from the bottle then wiped his mouth with the back of his hand. His figure was outlined in the light at his back, and to Rowan, he looked like a ghost or some kind of dark phantom.

Rowan shifted on his bed and the movement caught Sawyer's eye. He turned to Rowan and for a moment, Rowan thought he was going to throw the bottle at the window. But when he saw that it was Rowan, his shoulders relaxed some and he began to stumble over, still muttering to himself.

"You spyin' on me?" Sawyer asked, coming to a stop a couple feet from Rowan's window. His voice was low and his speech ran together, like the words were too big for his mouth.

"I was here first," Rowan responded quietly so his parents wouldn't hear.

Sawyer grunted and took another tug from the bottle. "Don't get smart with me, kid. Not tonight. I'm begging you."

From this distance, Rowan could smell the alcohol on his breath. It was a heavy stench, mixed with sweat and dirt. Sawyer's hair was matted and damp and he looked like he was panting heavily, as if he had just gone for a run.

"Are you OK?" Rowan asked, concerned.

Sawyer licked his lips and stared out at the darkness. "OK? Who the hell knows? It's been a night, I'll tell you that."

"I heard you fighting with Gayle earlier."

Sawyer looked sideways at him. "Yeah, I bet the whole damn park heard that. Damn bitch, always at the keyboard pushing my goddamn buttons. I swear to god, Row, never ever get married. I know you're sweet on that Brenda girl, but once you've had your fill, you gotta bail. It ain't worth it. As a man who's been there, I'll testify to that."

"What happened?" Rowan asked carefully, his voice a hush.

Sawyer twirled his fingers, as if that would explain everything. "Woman just has a mouth, that's all. She says things sometimes that make me feel two feet tall."

Rowan thought of his father and nodded. "I'm sorry. That sucks. She shouldn't do that."

Sawyer took another drink and then grinned, but it came out crooked. "Shit, look at me, getting a pep talk from a kid. I'm sorry Rowan, I shouldn't be laying this all out on you like this. It's not your problem."

Rowan sat up a little and propped his elbows on the window-sill. "We're friends right? Didn't you say that my problems were your problems? I don't mind, Sawyer. I'm sorry you're having a bad night. I am, too."

Sawyer rolled his shoulders. "Oh yeah? George blow a fuse when he saw your face?"

"That's putting it mildly," Rowan said. "He lost it. Gave me the cold shoulder all the way home then sat me down and basically told me I'm a bad person."

Sawyer bunched his face up. "Seriously? You? You're like the best kid I've ever met. What an asshole. He didn't hurt you, did he?"

Rowan looked away for a second and contemplated what he should say next. The more he thought about it, the more angry he got about the whole thing. He WAS a good kid. If Sawyer could see it then why couldn't his own father? What was wrong with him?

Maybe it's him that's bad. What kind of person hits their own kid? Why should you protect him? Why shouldn't you tell Sawyer? It's not your responsibility. He's the one that did it.

"He slapped me," Rowan said quietly. "I talked back and he just... slapped me. Right across the face." Rowan shook his head. "He's never done that before."

Sawyer suddenly became very still. "He did what?"

Rowan grunted. "I know. He's such a bastard. He's such a..." Rowan trailed off and became furious when he realized he was on the brink of tears again. He clenched his teeth.

"What is wrong with me, Sawyer?" he asked, his voice shaking. "You can tell me. You've always been honest with me so if you tell me there's something really wrong with me, then I'll believe you. I just don't know what anyone wants anymore. I try to stay out of trouble and make everyone happy, but I always end up getting the worst of it."

Sawyer stepped toward the window, so close Rowan could feel his breath on his face. It was hot and sour and smelled like rubbing alcohol.

"Nothing's wrong with you. Nothing at all. Don't you ever think that. These people around us, these parasites, they're the ones that are screwed up. Your dad, Gayle, those two fucks from earlier. They poke and they poke and they just expect you to fall in line and take it. But I'm done taking it, you hear me? I'm done. People like that shouldn't be allowed to walk the face of the earth. They shouldn't get to go around and treat folks like you and me badly. It's not right. I've been around people like that my whole life. Men. Women. Even before Gayle."

Sawyer sucked down another mouthful of whiskey and got a far-away look in his eyes. "One day I'll tell you about that. About Mia. When you're older. When you can grasp the extent and scope of how I've been wronged. This isn't some new rage I'm feeling, kid. It's been building for a long time and there's a lot of people who chipped in on the construction."

Sawyer took a long drink from the bottle before he continued. "Those little shits earlier? They're going to grow up to be people just like your dad. Condescending dogs who think they shit gold. My wife, Gayle? She thinks I don't do enough, that I'm not holding up my end of the marriage. She thinks she can just say whatever's on her mind without consequence. I mean, what kind of person thinks that way? We ALL have to atone for what we say and do. No one should be exempt. No one. And so when she starts mouthing off, I tend to get pretty fired up. I've been listening to it for years and that shit grinds on you like a worn-out brake pad until smoke is coming out of your ears. That's what you heard earlier. The smoke coming out of my ears."

Sawyer finished the bottle before he continued. "I think my marriage is over. It's right at the cusp. All it needs is one more push. I'm just too tired tonight to do it. God knows she won't. She has no problem running her mouth, but she'd never actually leave me. What the hell would she do? Huh? Go work some minimum-wage job and suck dick so she can afford rent?"

Sawyer looked up at Rowan. "Sorry."

Rowan just sat and absorbed it all like a sponge. No one had ever been so forward with him before. No one had spoken to him so honestly before.

I feel like I'm getting it straight for the first time in my life.

Sawyer chucked the bottle across the lawn. "I think it's time for me to go."

"Why is everything so bad, Sawyer?" Rowan asked suddenly, his voice edged with an almost infantile panic. "Why can't people just be nice?"

Sawyer met his eyes. "Because nice gets you slapped, kid, and the world doesn't give a fuck."

Rowan let his eyes sink, a weight pressing against his chest.

Sawyer smiled then, but the expression held no humor. "Don't worry, Rowan. It's not going to be like that for long. I promise you."

"What do you mean?"

Instead of answering, Sawyer turned away. "I'll see you soon, son. I got work to do."

Rowan sat and watched as Sawyer stumbled over to his truck, got in, and then drove off. The tail lights glowed red and then disappeared from sight as the Ford roared away.

To Rowan, they looked like eyes. Furious, bloody eyes.

CHAPTER 8

It wasn't until three days later that the knock came at the door. Rowan was lying on his bed, eating a peanut butter and jelly sandwich while idly flipping through his comic books. It was lunchtime and his mother could be heard in the kitchen making herself a grilled cheese. George was at work and the day was cloudy, threatening rain.

When Rowan heard someone knock on their door, he immediately thought it might be Sawyer. He hadn't seen him since the last time they spoke, and his truck had been absent from the neighboring lot.

Rowan sat up and pushed his plate away, wiping crumbs from his shirt. His bedroom door was open and he could see Rose set aside her skillet before going to the door. When she opened it, Rowan saw surprise ripple across his mother's face. From his spot on the bed, he couldn't see who it was, but his mother's voice was friendly and curious.

"Oh hi! How are you?"

A pause and then, as Rose's face dropped: "Hey, are you OK, honey?"

A second voice responded, but Rowan couldn't make it out. It sounded like another woman. He closed his comic books and stacked them on his nightstand, swinging his feet down onto the floor as he did so.

Rose waved someone inside and then a figure entered the trailer, shutting the door behind them.

Gayle. Not who I would have guessed, Rowan thought, staring down the hall at the two women.

Gayle looked like she was crying. Her arms were wrapped around herself and she wore a giant pair of dark sunglasses that she left on, despite the dim interior of the trailer.

"Sit down, sit down," Rose instructed, pulling out a kitchen chair for her. "Can I get you something to drink? Are you hungry? I can split this grilled cheese with you if you want?"

Gayle waved her away and slumped into the chair. When she spoke, her voice was thin and fragile.

"I'm so sorry to barge in on you like this, I just don't know who else to talk to right now."

"Oh sweetie, it's no trouble," Rose assured, taking a seat next to Gayle. "What happened? What's wrong?"

Gayle waved a hand helplessly. "Everything. Everything is wrong and I don't know what to do. I'm usually pretty good at keeping my business to myself, but things have never gone this far and I don't know what to do and I feel like I'm going crazy and—"

Rose put a hand on Gayle's arm. "Whoa, whoa, whoa, hon, slow down. Take a deep breath. Are you sure I can't get you some water? Beer?"

Gayle shook her head. "No, thank you. I feel so stupid right now, I really shouldn't be here."

Rowan saw his mother's face grow stern. "Ain't nothing wrong with asking for help if you need it. Now tell me—what happened?"

Instead of answering, Gayle took off her large sunglasses and Rowan saw his mother's face go pale. From where he sat, he could see some of the damage.

"My word, what in heaven's name—" Rose started, but Gayle cut her off.

"This happened three days ago—the day of the barbeque," Gayle said, her voice trembling. "This is why I wasn't there. Sawyer and I got into a big fight and his temper started to flare and once that happens there's just no stopping it. At least not lately. Then, after he got back, we had another row. He was drunk this time and what you're looking at is what's left of our fight."

Rose reached for her cigarettes and lit one before continuing. "I'm so sorry, hon. I had no idea. They can't do that to us. It's not right."

Gayle sat up a little straighter. "You can't tell anyone, Rose. You have to swear to me. If he found out I was talking to you...I don't know what he'd do. You can't say anything, please, I'm begging you—"

"OK, OK," Rose assured gently. "My lips are sealed. But Gayle, what he did to you is cruel. You do know that, right?"

"Of course I know that," Gayle said hurriedly. "I...I just need to learn to keep my mouth shut. It's just sometimes he says things to me that hurt so...so damn deep that I can't help myself. If I don't stand up for myself, then who will? I try to ease his temper as best I can, but that always makes it worse and I don't know what to do. It's like he wants to be angry with me sometimes, like all of his failures are somehow my fault."

Rose exhaled a plume of smoke. "Yeah, I've known a guy or two like that when I was younger. Sad little men with no aspirations and no motivation. But somehow that's *our* fault. That sound familiar?"

Gayle nodded. "Does it ever. He's never been this bad before though and that's what scares me. He's been drinking a lot lately and that just makes it worse."

"Yeah, but it gives them an excuse when they want to apologize," Rose said. She ashed her cigarette and then licked her lips. "What can I do to help, dear? Tell me."

Gayle drooped some in her chair. "I don't know. I'm so scared. I haven't seen him since that night."

"Wait, Sawyer's gone?"

Gayle nodded. "Yeah, after the fight he just stumbled out of the trailer and drove off. He hasn't been back since." She paused and twisted her hands together. "He's never done this before and it has me worried sick. I don't know if he's just on a bender or if he's gone for good. And if he is, then I don't know what I'm going to do. I don't make enough money to afford payments on the trailer and I don't know the first thing about—"

Rose cut her off. "Don't worry about that. I'm your neighbor and your friend. As long as that's the case then you have a place to stay."

Gayle wrung her hands together even tighter. "Oh Rose, I couldn't ask—"

"You're not asking, I'm offering. If he doesn't come back, then we'll take care of you. I'll take care of you. At least until you sort your mess out and are back on your feet. Deal?"

Gayle began to cry again. She reached out and took Rose's hand. "Thank you. I can't tell you how stressed out I've been about this. I'd repay you in any way I could."

Rose stubbed out her smoke. "Nonsense. There's no need. Just know that my door is always open to you."

Gayle smiled around her bruised face and took a deep breath. "There's more though."

Rose spread her hands. "Might as well get it all out then while we're here. You have my ear. Both of them."

Gayle fidgeted with the tablecloth as she spoke, her eyes focused on her hands. "It's about the night Sawyer left."

"What about it?"

"He was saying some things."

"What kind of things?"

"Things he shouldn't be saying. He was talking about how bad people are and how there's a lot of injustice out there and that I was a part of that."

"Well, isn't that ironic?"

Gayle looked up and met Rose's eyes. "Rose, he was talking about hurting people."

Rose's face grew serious, her mouth a thin white line. "Who?"

Gayle bit her lip, her voice low. "It didn't make any sense. He was talking about these two kids…"

"He wasn't talking about Rowan, was he?" Rose cut in sharply.

Gayle's head snapped up. "Oh, Lord, no. Never Rowan, he loves that boy. I think he wishes he was his father sometimes. No, Rose, I promise, he wouldn't touch a hair on that kid's head."

"Who then?"

"Well, at first I didn't know and I kind of brushed it off," Gayle continued. "After all, I had enough on my mind after that night. And

I had a lot to clean up. So I didn't really think much about it until this morning."

"What happened this morning?"

Gayle took a long, shuddering breath. "I was cleaning up the bedroom and I had the radio on. I heard on the news that someone's gone missing. A boy in town."

Rose's face went white. "What boy?"

"I don't know. They said his name is Cody Hillson. He's been missing since the night of the barbeque."

Rowan had been listening intently from his bed, his chest tightening with every word. When he heard Cody's name, his blood went cold and his skin turned gray.

Cody's....missing?

His pulse quickened and he leaned forward on his bed, making sure he caught every word.

Rose was silent for a moment before speaking. "I know him. Or at least, I've seen him around. I always thought he was a nasty boy, but that doesn't make this situation any less frightening. Are they sure he didn't just run away? He seemed like the type."

Gayle tapped on the table nervously with one hand. "I don't know. No one knows. He could have, I suppose, but the way Sawyer was talking..."

"You don't think he'd actually do something like that, do you?"

Gayle leaned forward on her elbows and covered her face with her hands, her voice strained. "I don't know, Rose. He's just not the same man I fell in love with all those years ago. He's so cynical now. So unpredictable. I don't know if I should say something or do something or what..."

"You mean go to the police?"

Gayle looked up from her hands. "Do you think I should?"

Rose exhaled slowly. "I don't think I can answer that for you. You know Sawyer better than anyone so I trust your judgment." Rose shook her head then. "I feel like I'm having an out of body experience. We just had you two over for dinner and I never would have suspected any of this."

"He's good at hiding things," Gayle said. "There's a lot about Sawyer he doesn't let the outside world see. He's a charming son of a bitch which gets him out of a lot of trouble. Or at least, it has in the past."

Rowan felt like his ears were burning. His mind was reeling and he couldn't seem to get his thoughts under control.

Do they really think Sawyer kidnapped Cody? He's got a temper, sure, but Sawyer is a decent person, he wouldn't actually go that far, would he?

And then he remembered how Sawyer had acted in the bathroom at the barbeque. How he had taken his belt off.

How he had practically begged Rowan for permission to *make things right.*

A slow smile spread across Rowan's face then.

Maybe he did do it. Maybe he did it to scare Cody so he'd stop being such a jerk to me.

His smile grew and he laid back down on his bed as the conversation in the kitchen began to wind down. He didn't pay any attention to the rest of it, his mind expanding upon the possibilities of what he had just heard.

How hilarious would that actually be, Rowan thought, lacing his hands behind his head. *I hope Sawyer* did *kidnap him. I hope he scared the crap out of that asshole.*

Rowan pictured Cody huddled away in some room, whimpering like a little baby, and he couldn't help but chuckle. It was a good feeling. Like something bad in the world had been erased and made clean again.

God, I hope he did it.

Rowan closed his eyes.

Would serve the bastard right.

CHAPTER 9

Rowan kept his head down over the next two days. The conversation between his mother and Gayle remained centered in his mind, replaying over and over again on loop. He heard his mother mention it in passing to George at one point, but no new information came from it. He kept his eyes peeled for Sawyer's red Ford, but it remained absent from the neighboring lot. Gayle didn't return to their trailer and he didn't see much of her either. He figured she had withdrawn into a state of heightened anxiety and he felt a little sorry for her.

George didn't seem particularly interested in his neighbors' state of affairs. He brushed it off as "none of his business" and went about his day. Rowan didn't have much interaction with him, but when he was around, Rowan could always feel his eyes on him. Like he was being studied and observed like an organism under a microscope. Knowing this, Rowan kept to himself and busied himself in his room. He read, watched TV, played video games, and thought a lot about Brenda. He wondered how she was doing, if she was thinking about him, and when he could see her next. He missed her.

I saved her, Rowan thought one night as he was lying in bed. *That's got to count for something, doesn't it?*

You also got your ass kicked. Not exactly boyfriend material, are you?

Sure, but maybe it was enough.

Right, and maybe she'll call you out of the blue and ask if she can kiss you.

Rowan turned over and faced the wall, sighing heavily.

I just hope she's OK. If she wants to kiss me, then I'll just have to wait for it.

He shut his eyes and tried to silence his thoughts. He wasn't really tired, but it was late and his parents had gone to bed two hours ago. He felt restless, like there were coils of energy in his stomach just begging to be burned off.

Rowan sighed again and flipped over onto his back. Thoughts of Brenda and Cody and his father waged war in his head for another hour, tormenting his mind which only begged for silence.

He jerked upright when someone began tapping on his bedroom window. It happened so suddenly that Rowan almost screamed, the intrusive noise breaking the quiet of his room. Heart in his throat, he turned to the window and peered out, chest thumping.

A shadow moved in the darkness and the tapping came again, along with a muted voice.

"Hey, kid, you awake? It's me."

Sawyer? Rowan thought, bewildered, mind racing.

"It's me, come on, open your window," the voice instructed quietly.

Trying to calm himself as best he could, Rowan rolled up onto his knees and pulled the window open. The warm summer night air rushed into the room and filled Rowan's lungs with relief.

Squinting, Rowan peered out into the darkness. "Sawyer?" he whispered.

Suddenly, a face filled the window and Rowan jolted back on his bed as his adrenaline spiked and he stifled a yelp before it could escape.

Sawyer grinned down at him, his dark hair falling into his eyes. "Hey buddy, long time no see."

Rowan put a hand to his chest, panting. "You scared me half to death! What are you doing out there?! Where have you been?!"

Sawyer's smile grew. "Just been living life, man, the way I always shoulda been. You been worried about me?"

"I mean, a little."

"That's sweet," Sawyer said. "But I didn't come by just to calm your troubled mind."

"You going home to see Gayle?"

Sawyer snorted. "God no. I have no desire to see that bitch right now."

"Why not?"

"Because I got bigger things going on," Sawyer pressed. "And I want you to come with me."

"What? Now?!"

"Keep your voice down," Sawyer hissed. "You want to wake your parents?"

Rowan looked over his shoulder at his bedroom door before continuing. "I can't leave, it's the middle of the night! My dad would kill me if he found out!"

"So let's make sure he doesn't," Sawyer said quietly. "Come on, it'll be fun. I want to take you night fishing. I told you I would and I meant it. Hop to it, kid, let's roll."

But Rowan remained where he was, his pulse finally slowing. "Hold on. This is crazy. Where the heck have you been? Gayle was over here a couple days ago crying her eyes out. She thought you were leaving her for good. She was saying a lot of bad things about you."

Sawyer's jaw tightened. "I bet she was. Women will say anything to get folks on their side."

Rowan bit his lip. "But her face...it looked bad. Really bad."

Sawyer sighed and ran a hand over his eyes. "Look, Rowan...you know that dog that attacked you?"

"Yeah?"

"What'd you do when it came for you?"

Rowan frowned. "I tried to run."

"And what'd you do when that didn't work?"

"I fought it."

Sawyer nodded. "Exactly. That's exactly what happened with Gayle. She attacked my person and all I did was fight against it. Same as you. Are you saying it's OK for you to act that way and not me? That doesn't seem fair."

"Well, n—no—" Rowan mumbled.

"Right. Of course not. That's because you're a smart kid and you know a thing or two about how the world works. I didn't mean to hurt

Gayle like that—just like you didn't mean to hurt that dog, but our backs were against the wall, weren't they?"

"I guess so…"

"So get some clothes on and let's go!"

Rowan still wasn't entirely convinced and thoughts of his father waking up kept him on his bed. "Can't we do this in the morning?"

"Shit no we can't," Sawyer said. "I don't want Gayle seeing me. If she sees me then she's going to want to talk and I'm just not there. Look man, I've stuck my neck out for you a couple times now and all I'm asking in return is for you to go fishing with me."

"Ah geez," Rowan mumbled worriedly.

Sawyer rested his forehead against the raised window. "Look Row, if you really don't want to, you don't have to. I was just asking. I know you've had a lot on your plate lately and I don't want to add to it. That's not what a good friend does."

"I guess I can go," Rowan finally said, looking up. "But you have to bring me back before my parents wake up. Otherwise we might as well go dig my grave right next to those dogs."

"Hell yeah," Sawyer whispered excitedly. "You're a real bowl of peaches, you know that kid? Swear to god, you just made my night."

"OK, OK, let me just put some clothes on and find my shoes. I'll meet you out front."

"I'll be there with bells on."

"No bells, you have to be quiet!" Rowan hissed, but Sawyer was already gone.

Rowan hurried to dress, his mind racing the whole time. He was acutely aware of his own heartbeat as he pulled on a shirt and slid into his jeans. Every tiny noise he made sounded like it was broadcasted through a megaphone, and he prayed his parents would remain asleep until his return.

This is crazy, what are you doing?

Rowan put his shoes on and went to his bedroom door.

Too late now.

Quietly, he slid out of his room and crept across the living room, his breath held prisoner in his throat. When he reached the front door, he bit his lip and slowly turned the knob. It groaned quietly in protest, but as he inched the door open, he knew he was in the clear. He had made it.

He slid out onto the front steps and shut the door behind him, taking his time so it wouldn't snap back and wake the entire world. When it clicked into place, he finally took a breath. He turned around to see Sawyer grinning in the moonlight before him.

"Nice work, Casper."

Rowan stepped down into the front lot. "Who's Casper?"

"He's a ghost," Sawyer explained quietly. "Because you were like a ghost just now? Never mind, come on, my truck's right over there."

"Where's the fishing gear?" Rowan asked as he began to follow Sawyer.

"It's in the truck already."

Rowan padded across the hard packed earth, sweeping his eyes across the trailer park as he did so. Everything was bathed in soft, milky moonlight, giving the dozens of trailers a haunted, glowing look. It was late enough where even the crickets had gone to sleep, leaving the night in a kind of still silence, interrupted only by the occasional breeze that shook the treetops of the surrounding wood.

When they reached Sawyer's truck, Rowan pulled the door open and took one last look at his trailer. He expected to see his father coming for him, his eyes sleep-crazed, his hair a wild nest. But everything remained dark and silent, allowing Rowan some mild relief.

As Sawyer started the Ford and pulled away, Rowan was struck with just how odd this whole situation was. He looked down at his feet and saw a half-empty bottle of whiskey lying on the floor along with an opened box of Pop-Tarts. He looked across at Sawyer and then out at the trailer park, the small units illuminated by the headlights as they passed them, headed toward the open road.

"Hand me one of those Pop-Tarts, pal," Sawyer said as they neared the park entrance. Rowan reached down and passed him a package, the last in the box. Sawyer tore it open and began to eat. He glanced over at Rowan half way through.

"You want one?"

"Nah, I'm OK."

"You're awfully quiet tonight. You still worried about getting in trouble?"

Rowan shrugged and stared out the window as they pulled out onto the main road. "I guess so."

Sawyer stuffed the rest of the Pop-Tart in his mouth. "Aw relax, man. Here, open up that bottle of whiskey at your feet."

Rowan bent down and picked up the bottle, feeling the contents slosh around. He unscrewed the cap and offered it to Sawyer.

Sawyer brushed crumbs from his shirt. "Why don't you have a sip? Don't worry, I won't tell anyone. It'll calm you down."

Rowan took a sniff and winced. "I don't think so. It smells terrible."

"Sure, but it'll make you feel great. Go ahead, you're old enough."

Reluctantly, Rowan placed the bottle to his lips and took a tentative sip. He immediately felt his gag reflex kick into high gear and he coughed violently, wincing.

"Oh my god, that's disgusting!"

Sawyer grunted and snatched the bottle from Rowan's hands. He took a long pull and then smacked his lips, keeping one hand on the wheel.

"The more you drink, the easier it gets. I was about your age when I started drinking and I thought the same thing. But I kept doing it. You know why? 'Cause the girls loved it. Thought it was cool. Suddenly they always wanted to hang out and I realized that if you got them drunk enough, they'd do anything with you. And I mean *anything*, kid."

"It still tastes gross," Rowan muttered, wiping his mouth.

Sawyer said nothing and took another gulp of whiskey. The road was completely empty this late at night and as Rowan watched Sawyer continue to drink, he was thankful they were the only travelers. Though he would never say it, he knew drinking and driving weren't a good combo.

Sawyer knows what he's doing. There's no one around and he doesn't seem drunk. Stop worrying so much.

Rowan returned to the window and watched as the moonlit fields blurred by. They were headed in the opposite direction of town, toward the wooded hills. Rowan hadn't been this way much because there wasn't much out here except for a few odd houses and snaking dirt roads. It was where the deep-country people lived. At least, that's what his dad always said.

"Where are we going exactly?" Rowan asked as they turned down a dirt road, headed further into the belly of the woods. A wall of dark trees lined either side of the road and the crunch of gravel growled beneath the tires.

"You'll see," Sawyer said, now quiet. He took another drink and Rowan watched.

Twenty minutes crawled by, the cab filling with silence. The moon filtered in through the trees overhead and splashed its fragmented light across the dusty road. They wound their way deeper and deeper into the forest, the truck bouncing and grunting across the potholes and washboard divots.

Finally, Sawyer slowed and turned, the headlights washing across a single mailbox at the end of a long driveway.

Rowan frowned. "I thought we were going fishing? Whose house is this?"

Sawyer turned the headlights off but continued to crawl up the gravel driveway. He leaned forward and squinted, relying on the moonlight to carve the way.

Rowan began to feel uncomfortable. He felt incredibly far away from home and no one knew where he was.

Stop being such a baby. You're always worrying and crying about something. Live a little, like Sawyer always says.

Sawyer stopped the truck and shut off the engine. In front of them, about ten yards away, stood a single story house. It was in terrible condition and the front porch looked about ready to cave in on itself. Old car parts littered the frayed front lawn, woven together by wild weeds and used tires. No light came from the windows.

"Whose house is this?" Rowan asked again, his stomach fluttering.

Sawyer took another gulp of whiskey, finishing the bottle. He tossed it onto the floor and pointed to the glove box.

"Open that. We're going to go see a friend of yours."

Rowan reached for the latch. "I don't have any friends, though."

Sawyer smiled and a trickle of whiskey ran down the corner of his mouth. He wiped it away and motioned toward the glove box. Rowan opened it and reached inside.

His fingers found something and he pulled it out. It was a gun. It surprised him so much he almost dropped it. He stared down at it and was shocked at how heavy it felt. It wasn't a big gun, just a short little revolver, but in that moment it felt like he was holding an anchor.

"Sawyer?" he asked, his voice quiet.

Sawyer took it from him and stuffed it into his waistband. He opened the door to the truck, letting in the cool night air.

"Come on. This'll be fun."

Rowan felt his stomach turn, but he stepped out into the darkness and quietly closed the truck's door. The woods around them pressed in tight, encircling the small lot. The tall, swaying trees seemed more like wary judges now, watching Rowan with a cautious eye.

He followed Sawyer toward the house, anxious and alert. He knew they were doing something they shouldn't be doing, but he didn't have the courage to stop it. Instead, he tugged on Sawyer's sleeve.

"Hey, I'm getting kind of freaked out."

Sawyer paused and crouched, facing Rowan. "We're going to play a little joke. That's all. I need you to play along, OK?"

"What joke? Whose house is this?" Rowan asked, wringing his hands together.

Sawyer grinned in the dim darkness. "It's Tyler's. He lives here with his old man. I've been trying to figure out where he lives for the past two days and I've finally nailed it down. Dumpy little place, ain't it?"

Rowan blinked, the answer not the one he expected. "Tyler? Really?" He shot a quick look at the surrounding treeline, the black wall of forest offering no answer. "But...why?"

Sawyer stood up then. "'Cause I'm tired of him pushing you around. We're going to play a little prank on him. Don't worry, we're not going to hurt him. I just want to scare him. Make sure he knows he can't mess with you anymore. Stop fidgeting, Row, just follow my lead and everything will be OK. This is going to be hilarious. Don't you want to give him a little payback for all the crap he's put you through?"

Rowan looked at the front of the house and studied its blank, lightless windows, his mind buzzing.

That does sound kind of fun. God knows he deserves it. Where's the harm in it? Don't you want him to stop bugging you all the time? And think about what he did to Brenda. You really going to let him just get away with that? He touched her. Touched her until she was crying.

The image of Brenda back in the church bathroom sent a bolt of fire up Rowan's spine and he curled his hands into fists.

His memory brought back the way she had cried, pleaded.

Bastard. Mean, stupid bastard.

Rowan nodded then and looked up at Sawyer. "OK. I'm in."

Sawyer clapped Rowan on the shoulder. "I knew you were a good dude. Piece of shit deserves to have his marbles rattled a little, doesn't he? Just follow my lead and play along. And be quiet, I don't want to wake his dad. Though word around town is that he's got a little bit of a drinking problem. Let's hope his pour was heavy tonight."

Crouched low, Rowan followed Sawyer toward the house. They crept up the front porch, the steps creaking loudly, but they were muffled some by the rustling foliage overhead. Sawyer reached for the front door and tested it. It opened without protest.

"Looks like we're in luck," Sawyer whispered. "Follow me. Quiet as a ninja now."

Together, they slid inside, closing the door at their backs. The interior smelled like rotten food and they waited for their eyes to adjust to the darkness, trying their best to block out the smell. Rowan rubbed his nose and grimaced.

No wonder Tyler is garbage, he lives in a dump.

When his eyes had sharpened, Rowan studied his surroundings. An old TV sat on a stand across from him, along with a coffee table stacked with beer bottles. To his left, against the wall, sat a battered couch that was slightly lit by the large bay window behind him. The kitchen was straight ahead, flanked on both sides by a hallway.

I would never want to live here. Not in a million years. I'd blow my brains out in two days.

Suddenly, Sawyer gripped Rowan's shoulder and pointed toward the couch on their left. Rowan squinted at it, trying to figure out what Sawyer was seeing. When he did, his heart leapt into his throat.

Tyler was lying fast asleep on it. He was on his side, facing them, his long hair spilling over his shoulders.

Sawyer motioned for them to creep forward. Rowan, heart thundering, did as he was told, careful not to knock over any of the beer bottles that ran from the coffee table down across the floor.

Slowly, Sawyer knelt down in front of Tyler. He reached for the gun and looked up at Rowan with a smile. Rowan stood paralyzed behind him, unsure what he was supposed to be feeling, all too aware of his drumming pulse.

Sawyer suddenly placed his hand over Tyler's mouth and placed the barrel of the revolver to the boy's head, directly between his eyes. Tyler awoke with a startled shake, his eyes snapping open in a panic. He tried to sit up, heaving himself in confusion, but Sawyer held him in place, his hand still firmly over the youth's mouth.

"Keep it down, buster," Sawyer whispered, his face inches from Tyler's. "It's just us. You remember me, don't you?" Tyler's eyes darted around in the darkness, wide and terrified, his throat trying to push out sound.

"You certainly recognize Rowan, right?" Sawyer continued, the gun locked to the boy's forehead. "Course you do. How could you forget?"

Rowan, while enjoying the fear emanating off of Tyler, remained silent, his thoughts locked in place behind a wall of uncertainty.

"We're going to go for a little ride," Sawyer pressed, his voice a hiss. "All you have to do is shut up and come along. If you behave and do as you're told then I won't hurt you. Can you do that for me, bud?"

Tyler's face was white and his eyes were practically crawling out of their sockets. He just stared at Sawyer, then at Rowan, as if unsure who he should focus on.

"I'm going to need some kind of confirmation," Sawyer said, pressing the gun a little harder into the boy's head. "Just nod that you understand. Nod if you'll keep your lips zipped. I don't want to wake your dad. That wouldn't be good for anyone. You see, I've had a couple drinks tonight and my trigger finger is a little loose right now. I wouldn't want there to be some kind of terrible accident. You catch my drift?"

And then, finally, Tyler nodded, as if the gravity of the situation had finally penetrated his mind.

"Good," Sawyer said, relaxing some. "Up you go then. Out the door. We'll be right behind you. And mind the beer bottles. Don't you ever clean up? This place is embarrassing."

Sawyer pulled Tyler up by his T-shirt and prodded him in the back with the gun towards the front door. Tyler stood on shaky legs, knees wobbling, his mouth half-open like he wanted to scream but couldn't find the breath. Even in the dim light, Rowan could see that Tyler had wet himself, a dark patch growing in the front of his basketball shorts.

"Eyes forward, dipshit," Sawyer growled. "The only thing behind you is me and Rowan and that should be enough to keep you moving. You've been a bad dude, teasing my friend here. That shit stops tonight. And I'm going to show you how. Now move."

Tyler did as he was told. It was clear that he was terrified and Rowan took some pleasure in the fact.

God knows he deserves it.

They reached the front door and Tyler opened it. Sawyer pushed him outside and down the front steps. The wood groaned and the night seemed to squeeze the oxygen from the air, the breeze dying as they walked down the driveway toward the truck.

As they did so, Sawyer looked over his shoulder and winked at Rowan, a small smile lining his lips.

Rowan felt himself relax some.

We're just scaring him. Calm down and enjoy it. He's getting what he deserves.

But when they reached the truck, Rowan's heart was still racing.

CHAPTER 10

Tyler sat wedged between Sawyer and Rowan, the shoddy house now in the rearview mirror. The cab reeked of piss and sweat, and Sawyer rolled down the window with a look of disgust.

"Did you seriously wet yourself?" he asked, turning on the headlights as they exited the driveway. He snorted. "That's honestly pretty pathetic. For someone who likes to push people around, you sure are a pussy. We haven't even done anything to you yet."

Tyler looked paralyzed, his face a pancake of quivering dough. He clutched his knees, his fingers digging into the skin. He stared straight ahead and seemed to be making some kind of sound deep in his throat.

"What's that now?" Sawyer asked, one hand on the wheel, the other prodding into Tyler's side with the gun. "You got something to say? Well go ahead, we're not going to wake anyone out here."

Tyler sputtered something, swallowed, and then tried again, his voice dry and raspy. "What are you going to do to me?"

Sawyer accelerated down the dark road, the trees whipping by on either side of the Ford. "Whatever the hell Rowan *wants* to do to you."

Tyler's eyes shifted to the right, meeting Rowan's. Rowan met them and then stared straight ahead. He had no idea what he was supposed to do. He hated Tyler, hated him for a lot of reasons, but he didn't want to seriously hurt him. Scare him, sure, but he thought they had already done a pretty good job of that.

Suddenly, Sawyer reached over and passed Rowan the gun. "Here, take this. Keep it trained on him. If he moves, shoot him in the leg."

"I'm not going to do anything," Tyler gasped quickly, his fingers digging deeper into his knees. "I promise I won't."

Rowan held the gun, noting its weight once again. He trained it toward Tyler's knee. He heard his captive struggle to remain under control, his legs shaking.

Doesn't feel good to be scared, does it? Rowan thought, finally feeling some of his anxiety ebb away. He had the gun now. He was in control. He knew how far to push things and when to stop.

"I'm sorry I've been mean to you," Tyler said, the words tumbling out of his mouth. "I swear I'll never bother you again. It was all Cody's fault. It was always his idea. I just went along with whatever he said."

Without warning, Sawyer backhanded Tyler across the mouth. Tyler let out a tiny squeak and clutched his nose, shrinking into himself, his eyes bulging.

"Don't you dare try to pawn off your actions on your friend," Sawyer growled, returning to the road. "I cannot *stand* that. Nothing makes you less of a man than to blame someone else for what you've done. That's what cowards do." Sawyer noted the wet stain on Tyler's pants and grunted. "Clearly you fit the bill."

"I'm sorry," Tyler moaned, beginning to cry now. "I'm really, really sorry Rowan."

Rowan gripped the gun tighter. "Shut up. Just shut up."

Sawyer looked across at him and grinned.

"Where are we taking him?" Rowan asked, his voice empty.

Sawyer turned on his blinker and took a left down another dirt road, the wilderness expanding before them beneath a dark curtain.

"There's a spot not too far from here. It's the perfect place to have a nice conversation about all this. Man to man. You just keep the gun on him until we get there."

Rowan watched Tyler out of the corner of his eye, noting how the frightened boy kept his attention on the gun. Rowan shifted it slightly, aiming it at Tyler's knee, and saw him recoil some.

Just like how Brenda recoiled from you the other day. Scary, isn't it?

"Ah shit," Sawyer muttered.

Rowan looked at him. "What's wrong?"

"I didn't bring any more whiskey. This is going to be a long night and I'll be damned if I don't have a drink in the holster. We're going to make a quick detour. There's a twenty-four-hour gas station about five miles from here that'll sell me some. Won't take but a second."

Rowan eyed the empty bottle as his feet from earlier. "That wasn't enough?"

"You sound like Gayle," Sawyer said evenly.

"Don't let me stop you," Rowan said, shrugging. But inside, he squirmed a little. He could already tell that Sawyer was a little too loose, the truck swaying slightly down the abandoned dirt road, getting a little too close to the endless trees that lined it.

At this point, what does it matter? he thought. *This whole night is starting to feel like a dream.*

Sawyer turned right at the next intersection, the deep country unfurling even further. They passed a couple odd houses that were mostly dark—small ratty shelters that didn't look much better than Tyler's. The moon struck them from overhead as they passed, spilling its indifferent light across their dirty windows, illuminating them for a brief moment before the truck roared by. The wind that whipped through Sawyer's open window smelled of pine and dirt, almost completely eliminating the foul stench that emanated off of Tyler.

After about ten minutes, the trees cleared some and they hit asphalt, the truck bouncing roughly over the threshold. As they did so, Sawyer pointed out past the sprawling fields of wild hay before them.

"There she blows."

A single gas station stood along the side of the road, surrounded by empty fields and seemingly endless foothills. To Rowan, the neon lights were like some kind of reward for making it out of the woods.

Welcome back to society. Have a Twinkie.

In the far distance, far beyond the gas station, Rowan spotted lights from the next town over. He had only been there once, years ago, and couldn't remember the name. As Sawyer pulled in, Rowan suddenly remembered he was holding a gun. He pulled it away and let his arm sink in between the door and the seat.

Sawyer parked at the opposite end of the gas station, the light from inside spilling out onto the dirty lot, and he shut the engine off.

"I'll be gone just a second. You boys need anything? You want a soda, Rowan?"

Rowan shook his head. He was thirsty, but for some reason he just ignored it. Sawyer looked at Tyler, grinning.

"What about you, champ? Want me to see if they have any clean undies for you?"

Tyler just stared at his hands, his eyes watering.

"Doesn't seem too confident tonight, does he Row?"

Rowan glanced at Tyler. "Doesn't seem like a lot of things."

Sawyer opened his door and stepped out of the truck. He turned around and shot a finger toward Tyler. "Don't forget that while I'm gone, Rowan still has the gun. I know you think you can pick on him, but my man here is cold-blooded. He'll shoot you if you try anything. I've seen him in action. Dude took out a wild dog with his bare hands. Ask him about it while I'm gone. He can tell you how he crushed its skull with a rock."

Sawyer double-tapped the side of the truck, smiled, and then shut the door. Rowan watched as he went inside.

The silence in the cab grew between Rowan and Tyler, as if they were waiting for the other one to shatter the growing ice. Rowan kept his mouth shut, letting the cold thicken and expand, hardening his resolve to keep his cool.

It was Tyler who finally broke, his voice a shaking shudder. "D—d—did you really kill a dog with a rock?"

Rowan stared out the windshield. "Yep."

Tyler swallowed, as if paralyzed in place. "Please let me go."

"No."

Tyler looked at Rowan and Rowan could feel his eyes burning into the side of his face, melting some of the ice. "He's going to hurt me. I just know he is. I know you're not a bad kid and I know I've been a jerk to you. I'm sorry, I really am, but he scares the shit out of me. *Please.*"

Rowan felt sick, the gun slick in his grip. "Shut up."

Suddenly, from out of the corner of his eye, Rowan spotted another car approaching the gas station from the opposite town. When he realized what he was looking at, his eyes grew wide.

"Oh no."

Tyler's head whipped around and when he saw the car, he leaned forward a little. "Is that a cop?"

Rowan felt a buzzing sensation crawl up his throat and he began to panic as he watched the squad car pull into the gas station.

No, no, no, oh no.

The car parked at the far end of the building and shut off its engine. A door opened and a big man stepped out. He looked to be about fifty, and he sported a graying goatee. He took his police cap off and wiped sweat from his forehead.

Tyler opened his mouth, but Rowan, without thinking, jammed the nuzzle of the gun into Tyler's side.

"Not a word," Rowan hissed, his heart racing. "Let him go inside. I'll shoot you if you don't. I'll kill you like I did that dog."

The words felt like vomit coming out of his mouth. He didn't mean what he was saying, couldn't even stomach the idea of shooting Tyler, but he was suddenly extremely scared.

I'm taking part in an active kidnapping. If that cop comes over here and figures that out, then I'm going to jail. Or worse.

Tyler slammed his mouth shut so hard his teeth clicked. He looked down at the gun pressed into his side and then turned his pale, sweating face to Rowan.

"You wouldn't do that. You're not a bad guy."

"Brenda wasn't a bad person either," Rowan forced, begging Tyler to believe his bluff. "If you call for help, you're going to get shot. If you keep your mouth shut then I promise I won't let Sawyer hurt you. He does what I want. He's my friend." Rowan felt like he was going to throw up. His eyes were glued to the cop who was now walking around his squad car toward the entrance of the gas station. His eyes reached past the double doors and he paused to appraise the red Ford.

"He sees us," Tyler gasped, his voice hopeful.

Rowan shifted the gun in his hand so that Tyler's body blocked it from the cop's sight. He pushed it harder into his side, earning him a grunt of pain.

The cop spotted the two boys sitting in the cab and he frowned. He put his cap back on and began to walk over.

No, no, go away! Rowan's mind screamed. *Go inside, please just go inside!*

But the policeman didn't stop. He was ten yards away now, his head cocked to the side to look in through the windows, getting a better view of the two boys.

"Don't say anything stupid," Rowan whispered in a frenzied panic, his ears thundering with the sound of his own heartbeat. Sweat beaded across his forehead and the back of his neck felt hot and sticky.

What am I supposed to do!? Oh God, what am I supposed to do!? Where are you Sawyer!?

The officer was five yards away from the window when Sawyer exited the gas station. Rowan saw him freeze, practically dropping the plastic bag in his hand.

"Can I help you?" he called out.

The cop spun on his heel and studied Sawyer for a moment before jerking his thumb over his shoulder at the two boys.

"They with you?"

Sawyer stayed where he was, his face transforming in an instant. "Yep! Got my boy in there with his friend."

"Little late to be driving them around, isn't it?" the cop asked, taking a quick look back into the truck. Rowan met his eyes and forced himself to calm down. The last thing he wanted was to show just how terrified he was.

Sawyer cleared his throat. "Yeah, you're telling me. My boy's friend here was sleeping over at our place and he got sick. He started puking everywhere, his stomach was killing him, the whole nine yards. So, I figured the best thing to do was to get him some ginger ale." Sawyer then reached into the plastic bag and held up a soda.

"That so?" the cop said, placing his hands on his hips. "You mind if I see some identification?"

Sawyer nodded enthusiastically. "Sure, sure." He reached for his wallet. "What's all this about, if you don't mind my asking? We haven't done anything wrong, have we? Is there a curfew in place I don't know about?"

The cop took Sawyer's license and examined it. "No, but there's a missing person's case over in the next town. Some kid has gone and vanished. We're supposed to be keeping our eyes open. You understand."

"Of course. I heard about that. Terrible, isn't it?"

"Sure is."

Sawyer shifted the bag in his hands. "Look, I'm just trying to do right by these kids. My wife, the boy's mother, left us about three months ago and it's been rough ever since. Just up and left without a word, can you believe that? It broke my kid's heart and damn near tore mine out. I haven't seen my son happy since then. I don't blame him. I thought maybe having one of his friends over would cheer him up, but now his friend's puking and…" Sawyer trailed off, his voice shaking toward the end. He looked down at his feet and pressed his fingers into his eyes. "I'm sorry. I shouldn't bother you with this shit. You're just doing your job. I'm sorry, sir."

The cop studied Sawyer for a moment and Rowan saw him relax some, a slight lowering of the shoulders.

"My wife left me a year ago," the cop said suddenly. "Married twenty-four years and then she goes and runs off with our neighbor. Left me and my three girls high and dry."

Sawyer looked up, his face in mock anguish. "You gotta be fuckin' kidding me."

The cop waved Sawyer's license. "Let me just run this and then I'll let you be on your way." He turned then to Rowan and Tyler. "Are you boys good?"

Rowan nodded, but Tyler just stared at his knees, his jaw clenched, his face slick with sweat.

"I'm afraid he puked on the way over here too," Sawyer said, eyeing Tyler. "Poor guy can barely move without getting nauseous."

The cop nodded. "OK, just give me two minutes."

He turned back to his car and walked past Sawyer. Sawyer strode to the truck and pulled the door open. With his back to the cop, his face changed in an instant.

"One peep out of you and I'll slit your fucking throat, do you understand me?" he hissed, inches from Tyler's face. He pressed the plastic bag into his lap. "Rowan, make sure he does as he's told."

Before Rowan could respond, Sawyer turned around and walked back toward the police car, leaving the door of the truck open. Rowan felt the night air creep in, cooling the sheen of sweat that clung to his flushed cheeks. He felt like he couldn't breathe, every heartbeat an exclamation mark across his eyes.

The cop finished running Sawyer's license and handed it back to him. "Alright, you're all set. Have a good night now. Get those boys home safe."

Sawyer stuffed his wallet back into his pocket. "Yes sir. Thank you. Drive safe."

And then he about-faced and marched back to the Ford. He climbed in and shut the door. He said nothing as he started the engine, keeping one eye trained on the police car. He backed up and then pulled out onto the main road, headed back toward the woods. When they had made it a couple miles, Sawyer finally exhaled, rolling his window down to let in the breeze. The night blurred past, silent as ever.

"Well that was a close call, wasn't it?" he half-laughed, leaning his head back against the headrest with one hand on the wheel.

Rowan finally pulled the gun off of Tyler and let out a shuddering exhale. His throat felt like it was wrapped in a hangman's noose.

Tyler put his hands over his face and began to cry.

Sawyer ignored him and reached into the plastic bag, pulling out a bottle of whiskey. He popped the top and took a long, gasping drink. He sighed and wiped his mouth, his mood returning.

"That's better," he grinned. He looked over at Rowan. "You good, man?"

"I think so."

"Fantastic. We got a night ahead of us, let me tell you."

Rowan looked at Tyler, whose shoulders shook as he cried. "Where are we taking him?"

Sawyer took another gulp of whiskey. "Where all bad kids go."

CHAPTER 11

Rowan didn't know how much time had passed before they turned off the dirt road and wound their way down another—snaking them through the claustrophobic trees beneath the radioactive moon. It couldn't have been more than fifteen minutes since they left the gas station. When Sawyer parked the truck in front of a dumpy little house, Rowan felt his nerves begin to spark once again.

The small house before them looked like it had suffered a fire recently. The roof appeared charred but intact, a layer of dark soot painting the frayed shingles. The big window in the front was cracked, a spiderweb that ran the length of it. The forest surrounding the meager shack was tight around its edges, nearly burying it from sight.

Sawyer capped his bottle of whiskey and climbed out. "Come on, let's go inside. Tyler, bring that plastic bag with you. There's some goodies in there still."

Tyler looked pleadingly at Rowan before sliding out of the truck after him. Rowan waited for Tyler to go first, his shoulders drooping in despair. Rowan held the gun tightly as he followed him, scanning the driveway at his back.

We're out deep. No one could possibly find us all the way out here.

Sawyer mounted the front steps and then waited for Tyler and Rowan to join him. He took the bag from Tyler and then motioned toward the door, his voice noticeably slurring now.

"Go on. In."

Tyler looked like he was going to wet himself again as he reached for the knob. He opened the door and it took a push to get him inside. He whimpered and stumbled into the darkened interior. Rowan watched as he was swallowed up before following, his stomach squirming.

Once all three were in the house, Sawyer shut the door and flicked the light switch along the wall. A single exposed bulb blinked to life, painting the interior in a urine-tinted yellow bath.

"The old bitch still has power," Sawyer grunted. "Thought for sure it wouldn't work this time."

Rowan's eyes swept across the filthy house. The hardwood floors were scuffed and rotten, the walls were stained and sported holes, there was no furniture to speak of, and the dark kitchen in front of him, just off the living room, was a black hole, an open mouth.

"This time?" Rowan asked quietly. "You've been here before? Whose house is this?"

Sawyer smiled. "Hell if I know. But I got a surprise for you."

"What do you mean?"

"Why don't you give me that gun first?"

Rowan stared down at the revolver and then handed it to Sawyer, feeling as if he shouldn't, but knowing he didn't have much of a choice. Sawyer took the gun and stuffed it into his waistband.

"What's the surprise?" Rowan asked then, his voice sounding suddenly very far away.

Sawyer grinned and walked across the room and into the kitchen. He stared at something Rowan couldn't see and then motioned with his hand.

"Come on. Papa's back. Come say hi to your friends."

Rowan felt his blood begin to curdle as something stirred from the darkness, a scuffling across the linoleum floor. Sawyer stepped back into the living room, motioning with his hand as he did so.

"Shit," Rowan hissed suddenly as his eyes met the figure. His stomach plummeted and his chest tightened.

Tyler's eyes went wide and he sank to his knees, wailing. "Oh no, no, no, no…"

It was Cody. He was naked and covered in filth. His hair hung ragged and his skin was pale, almost blue. His eyes were wide open and terrified, red-rimmed and haunted. He crawled on his hands and knees and Rowan saw that he had a chain around his throat, keeping him low to the ground, the end secured to something in the kitchen.

"C—Cody?" Rowan sputtered, his mind in full shock.

Sawyer grabbed the chain around Cody's throat and rattled it. "Say hi to Rowan! Go on!" Sawyer kicked him in the rear, sprawling the naked boy out across the floor.

Cody looked up, tears running down his dirty face. "R—Rowan? Is that you?" His voice was weak and horrified.

Sawyer chuckled and looked at Rowan. "Surprise! Oh boy, if I had a picture of your face right now I'd treasure it forever. Not what you were expecting, huh?"

Rowan couldn't tear his eyes off of Cody. "Why...why is he like this?"

Sawyer stared down at the naked boy. "'Cause this is where he belongs. Exposed and crawling across the floor like the little bitch insect he is. I scooped him up right after the barbeque. Can you believe he was still following Brenda around? Even after what he did to her? If I hadn't, I'd bet you anything he would have gone after her again."

This isn't right, Rowan's mind warned. *This is cruel.*

Cody curled into himself, his voice a wailing plea. "I wasn't going to hurt her, I promise! I'll never look at her again if you let me go! Please!"

Sawyer curled his lip. "Shut the fuck up. Remember what happened last time you wouldn't keep your mouth shut?"

Cody suddenly slammed his teeth together so loud that Rowan was sure he had broken a few of them. Sawyer winked at Rowan.

"Kids like him are just like women. Only one way to keep 'em quiet."

Tyler's voice suddenly cut through the air, a shrill howl. "I want to go home! Please take me home! Please!"

Sawyer dragged his teeth across his lower lip and shook his head. "Swear to god these little retards never learn." He walked across the room and leaned down into Tyler's face. "What did I JUST tell Cody about staying quiet? Huh!? Speak!"

Tyler was huddled against the wall with his knees drawn up. He was crying into his arms and refused to look up, his whole body shaking.

"We can do it that way," Sawyer said quietly, his voice like venom. He set down the whiskey bottle and upended the plastic bag. A bag of chips and a ginger ale fell out, rolling across the floor.

"Here we go, champ," Sawyer said darkly, stepping forward. He pulled the plastic bag over Tyler's head and jerked him up into a standing position.

Then he began to suffocate Tyler. He held the bag tight against the thrashing boy's face while keeping him in place with his free arm. Tyler screamed in terror and then the plastic entered his mouth, reducing him to wheezing gasps. His feet drummed against the floor and somewhere in the chaos, Cody was crying from the kitchen.

"One Mississippi...two Mississippi," Sawyer laughed, jerking Tyler's head back roughly. "Come on, buddy, I know you got at least thirty in you!" He tightened his grip across Tyler's body as the boy continued to jerk and spasm.

"Three Mississippi!"

Rowan felt like the shack was spinning, his head filling with a swaying dizziness. His eyes were wide as he watched, his heart crashing into his rib cage.

He's killing him.

"Four Mississippi!"

The noises coming from the white plastic bag were more animal than human now.

"Five Mississippi! This is pathetic, you gotta breathe, champ, breathe!"

He's killing him.

"Six Mississippi! Don't wimp out, you can do it!"

Tyler, in his panic, was expending all the remaining air he had at an alarming rate. The bag frantically pulsed and retracted in great, whooping pulls.

"Seven Mississippi!"

"Stop it!"

Sawyer paused, his head slowly turning to meet Rowan.

"He's going to die!" Rowan pleaded, his head thundering.

Sawyer blinked, as if remembering that Rowan was there. He looked down at his captive, at the shuddering plastic bag pulled over his head, and then he grunted, releasing Tyler.

Tyler collapsed to the floor, banging his head against the wall as he did so. He ripped the bag off his face and rolled onto his back, sobbing, his chest rising and falling, mouth agape.

Rowan felt something ripple through his body and he shivered. He looked at Sawyer who was staring at Tyler.

"Barely made it to seven," Sawyer said, disappointed. "Guess I shouldn't be surprised, considering you're a pant-wetter." He then looked at Rowan and curled a finger at him. "Come here. I need to talk to you. In private."

Rowan shuffled over to the corner of the room, leaving Tyler weeping and gasping on the floor. Sawyer picked up his bottle of whiskey and took a quick drink before placing a hand on Rowan's shoulder. He leaned down close and Rowan was blasted with a gust of alcohol-soaked breath.

"What are you doing?" Sawyer whispered, shooting a peek over Rowan's shoulder to make sure Tyler wasn't attempting an escape.

Rowan looked down at his feet. "I thought you were going to kill him. I freaked out."

Sawyer grinned and his eyes seemed to float in their sockets, his drunkenness becoming more apparent. "Come on man, you gotta trust me. I told you we're just scaring them. Trust me, after tonight they're not going to bother you or your little girlfriend ever again. But you gotta help me sell this. You gotta get hard, dude. Grit up."

Rowan suddenly felt very tired. "I know, I'm sorry. But I think we've scared them enough. I mean look at them. Don't you think we should take them back?"

Sawyer took another pull of whiskey, his eyes going dark. "No. No way. Not yet."

Rowan wrung his hands together. "But what if someone finds out? Aren't we going to get in trouble?"

"Who th—hell is going to find out?" Sawyer grunted, his words slurring some.

Rowan looked over his shoulder at Cody, who lay chained to the kitchen floor. "People are looking for him. He's been gone a couple days now."

"I know, I was the one who scooped his ass," Sawyer said.

Rowan's mind reached back to the conversation his mother Rose had with Gayle. He bit his lip. "Remember how I told you Gayle came over and talked to my mom? Remember how I said she was saying all these bad things about you?"

The creases around Sawyer's eyes grew edges. "Yeah, what of it?"

"Well, she was talking about how Cody went missing. I don't know how, but she thought you might have done it."

Sawyer gritted his teeth. "Woman always had a gossip problem. Never knew when to keep her goddamn mouth shut."

Rowan pressed ahead. "She was wondering whether she should go to the police about it."

Sawyer's eyes suddenly snapped into place, his face centering. "What?"

Rowan shrugged, feeling sick. "She was just talking about it. I don't know if she actually did anything. But if she did, then the cops are going to come looking for you. And if they find you here, with Cody...and Tyler..."

Sawyer suddenly threw the bottle of whiskey across the room, shattering it against the far wall. Shards of glass exploded onto the floor, showering Tyler as he whimpered in fear. Rowan jumped and stepped back, his face going slack, his stomach rolling.

Sawyer clenched his jaw and his hands curled into fists. He breathed through his nose like a rabid dog, his teeth grinding behind his thin lips.

When he spoke, it was like steam being released from a great machine. "Are you telling me that my own wife snitched on me?"

Rowan suddenly felt terrified, like this piece of information should have remained buried beneath his tongue. He shook his head violently and raised his hands defensively.

"She was just talking, Sawyer. I don't think she did anything. She was just upset or something."

Sawyer stared out the dark window, his voice dangerously low. "My own wife turning traitor on me." He looked at Rowan, his eyes sparking. "Jesus Christ, kid. I mean Jesus H. *Fuck*." He placed a fist over his heart, his face furious. "That one burns. That one burns all the way through. She's gone and done the lowest of the low. She's turned her back on the one person she ain't supposed to. After all I've done for her, she goes to your mom and talks about snitchin'." Sawyer turned away again, exhaling spittle. "Oh Gayle, you got it coming, bitch. You got it coming hard."

Before Rowan could speak again, Tyler reared his head up from the floor, his voice a quivering plea.

"P—p—please take me home. I've learned my lesson, I swear!"

Sawyer zeroed in on the trembling boy and Rowan saw rage ignite across the man's features like wildfire. He stormed over to Tyler and grabbed him by the scruff of his shirt. He hauled him to his feet, his voice like iron.

"Take your clothes off and stop whimpering like a little pussy."

Tyler's eyes grew wide, horror rippling across his face. He shook his head, crying, as if denying what had been demanded of him.

Sawyer snarled at this and raised his hand, only to bring it down a second later, slapping Tyler so hard that he dropped to the floor once more. Sawyer stood over him, panting, chest heaving, his voice like burning coal.

"Do as you're told or I swear to god, I'll fuck the teeth right out of your face. You got that, *buddy*?"

Crying openly, cheek glowing, Tyler slowly began to pull his clothes off. Rowan almost couldn't watch, his chest fluttering with terrified anxiety.

I have to stop this. This is only going to get worse if it keeps going. He looked at Sawyer who towered over Tyler, watching as the young boy pulled off his pants. *He's like a train running out of track. I have to slow him down and get us out of here. But how? What am I supposed to do!?*

Tyler lay curled up in a ball, shivering, his bare chest and legs lined with goosebumps. Sawyer prodded him with his boot.

"Hey jackass, are you stupid? I said take your clothes off. That means everything."

Squeezing his eyes shut, Tyler slowly reached down and peeled off his underwear, crying the whole time. When he was completely exposed, he quickly covered his nakedness and shrunk into himself, sobbing.

Sawyer chuckled. "Yeah, I'd hide that pathetic thing, too. You talk like you got a ten-incher down there, but I guess the truth comes out, huh dipshit? No wonder you go around bullying kids. You got nothing down there. Hell, I'm surprised you weren't confused for a girl at birth."

Suddenly, Cody's voice echoed from the kitchen, a rasping plea. "I need...something to drink...please...oh *please*..."

Rowan looked at him, his eyes traveling over his bluish skin and grime smeared face. He saw the defeat in the boy's eyes, the desperation, and it made him feel absolutely disgusted in himself.

He's here because of you.

Rowan bent down and picked up the bottle of ginger ale that had rolled across the floor. He walked it over to Cody and knelt down.

"H—here..." he offered, extending it.

Cody looked up at him and their eyes met, a brief clash of hatred and gratitude, and then Cody accepted the Coke gratefully, hands shaking.

But before he could take a drink, Sawyer strode forward with a vengeance and booted the bottle away, catching the side of Cody's face in the process. Cody cried out, his body flopping across the floor, his hands clutching his cheek.

"That's not for him!" Sawyer bellowed, panting. He looked down at Rowan and then grabbed him, dragging him across the room and shoving him into the wall.

"What the hell is the matter with you, dude?" Sawyer hissed, shoving an angry finger into Rowan's chest. "I've worked my ass off setting this up for you and you're playing Mother fucking Mary with the bastards who beat you up. I can't believe I have to say this, but *what the fuck*?"

Rowan fought for his voice, shock roaring through him like a current. He could feel tears forming behind his eyes, the sudden outburst startling him.

"I'm sorry," Rowan whispered, his voice cracking. "I'm sorry, Sawyer. I don't think I want to do this anymore. This is really freaking me out."

"What are you TALKING about!?" Sawyer yelled into his face, slamming his fist into the wall by Rowan's head, his patience burning away in an instant. "I did this for you! I stuck my neck out 'cause I care about you! And now you're saying you don't want this? Are you serious right now? Please, tell me I'm hallucinating, because this really doesn't sound like the gratitude I deserve."

"I don't want to hurt them anymore," Rowan begged, his eyes beginning to mist. "Please, can we just go home?"

Sawyer stared at him for a long moment, his eyes so intense Rowan thought he'd catch fire.

And then, when Sawyer did speak, it was low and cold, like an arctic wind. "You're turning on me, aren't you?"

Rowan blinked, panicked. "What? No, of course not!"

Sawyer stood up, his voice dangerously cool. "You're just like her. You don't trust me anymore, do you? You're on their side, aren't you? After everything they've done to you…" Sawyer trailed off shaking his head. "After all I've done to help you, this is where you fall." Sawyer suddenly leaned down, his lips pulled back. "Hell, I've treated you better than your own father has."

"Sawyer I—"

"When have I done you wrong?" Sawyer cut in. "I've watched your back, helped you, listened to you vent when no one else would, hell, I even saved you from an ass kicking and yet…" Sawyer shook his head slowly. "You're on their side, aren't you?"

"You've been really nice to me," Rowan pleaded, his throat dangerously tight. "And I just want to go home and pretend none of this happened. *Please.*"

Sawyer sighed then, a great, heaving breath. He ran his hands down his face and stared out the dark window. Rowan watched him, feeling his heartbeat tick away the seconds.

Then, without warning, Sawyer pulled the revolver from his waistband, pointed it at Tyler, and shot him in the face.

The gunshot sounded like a cannon going off in the enclosed space and Rowan jumped and fell back against the wall. Tyler's head whipped back as a dark hole suddenly exploded beneath his left eye, spraying blood across the room. The smell of gunsmoke immediately filled the air and somewhere in the buzzing haze, Cody began to scream.

Rowan stood paralyzed against the wall, his heart crashing into his ears, his chest rising and falling like crashing waves of ice. His eyes were huge and the world swam, the room blurring and then refocusing.

He stared at Tyler's corpse, the details of his shocking execution burning into his mind like fire ants. Blood ran in streaks down the wall and pooled beneath the still body. It expanded, as if reaching for Rowan, calling to him.

Suddenly Rowan couldn't breathe. His throat closed up and he collapsed to the floor, grasping at his neck, begging for oxygen. It felt as if his entire body was being squeezed by some cosmic vice.

"Calm down," Sawyer said from the center of the room, his voice completely devoid of emotion. "Take a breath, kid, Jesus."

*Can't...get...air...*Rowan thought frantically. He felt like his eyes would pop out of his head, an immense pressure building in his skull.

Panic attack....having...panic...attack...

Rowan forced himself to slow down, shutting his eyes so that he wouldn't have to see the horror that had just unfolded before him. He focused on his breathing, begging his body to cooperate, but in the darkness he saw Tyler's head whip back, the blood splashing from the exit wound.

He killed him.
Breathe.
He killed him.
You have to breathe.
He shot him.
In...and out...

When Rowan finally managed to choke down a couple lungfuls of air, he peeled his eyes open to see Sawyer standing in front of Cody. He was pointing the gun at him, his body relaxed and slumping some, like he was offering the boy something to eat.

Rowan reached up, trying to find the oxygen to stop this, his mind blitzing in a panic once more. But after a moment, Sawyer dropped the gun and shook his head.

"No. You don't get it so easy. Not after what you said to me. Not after what you *called me*. Don't think I've forgotten about that."

Cody was weeping into his arms, the chain clinking around his throat as he tried to pull his knees up into himself.

Sawyer stuffed the pistol back into his waistband and went behind Cody, disappearing into the gloom of the kitchen. Rowan stayed where he was, feeling as if his body was drying out and then cracking into pieces. His ears still rang from the deafening gunshot and his hands shook as he tried to steady himself against the wall. His mind roared like a storm, screamed at him, howled in the madness.

And Tyler remained dead on the floor.

Sawyer returned a moment later holding the end of Cody's chain. He jerked it up, forcing the naked youth to his feet in a gasping rush. Rowan saw Cody's legs were shaking as he stood, his dirt-stained face streaked with tears. He looked pitiful and completely broken.

"Come on, both of you," Sawyer said, headed for the front door. "We're going to take a little walk."

But Rowan didn't move, his body refusing to cooperate. His mind was blaring, forcing all thought from it.

Sawyer opened the door and looked across the room at Rowan. "If you don't come with me then I'm going to run him over with my truck as slowly as I can."

The threat of violence acted as a jolt of electricity, forcing Rowan to comply, his limbs stiff and janky, as if this were the first time he was using them. He stared at Cody's back as he followed them outside, the night air swallowing them up once more.

*Help us...please...*Rowan thought in anguish. *God, if you're listening, then please get me out of here. Please...*

Sawyer walked to the back of his pickup and stuck his arm over the side. When he pulled it back, Rowan saw that he now carried a tire iron. He yanked at Cody, leading them toward the backyard. Rowan followed, stumbling and tripping, his head thundering. Cody whimpered and continued to cry, a sound so desperate it made Rowan wish he were dead.

"I promised you we'd go fishing tonight, didn't I?" Sawyer called from ahead, leading them into the woods.

Rowan didn't respond, his feet moving on their own. He didn't know what to do, how he was supposed to stop this expanding nightmare. He wrapped his arms around himself as the woods engulfed him, praying more fervently than he ever had before.

They passed through the trees, the dark woods blurring together in an endless stretch, unfurling before them with nauseous consistency. Roots and small rocks threatened to trip Rowan multiple times, and he watched as Cody struggled to remain upright in front of him, the underbrush brutalizing his bare flesh.

"There's a pond back here," Sawyer called from the front. "I found it the first time I stumbled on that abandoned cabin. It's beautiful at night, you two are in for a real treat. There's even a little boat we can go out in. I don't know who left it there on the shore, but the thing should float." He looked over his shoulder at Rowan. "It should serve our purpose at least." He smiled then and Rowan felt a chill run up his spine.

After a couple minutes, they breached the treeline and found themselves on the bank of a small pond. It was about a hundred yards to the opposite bank and the still waters glowed beneath the pregnant moon. A gentle breeze tickled the treetops, filling Rowan's head with an earthy aroma, the surface of the pond rippling quietly.

Sawyer pulled Cody forward until he was standing next to him. He threw an arm over the naked boy's shoulder, sighing.

"She's something, ain't she? I'm not much of a water man myself, but even I can appreciate a sight like this." Sawyer looked back at Rowan. "Get up here and look at this!"

Rowan stayed where he was, his mind in overdrive, the smell of the woods and water turning his stomach.

Sawyer gripped the back of Cody's neck and squeezed hard enough that Cody whimpered.

"I said get over here, Rowan."

It wasn't an invitation, it was a demand. Rowan scurried over to their side, keeping his eyes on the ground.

"That's better," Sawyer said, his teeth gritted. "Wouldn't want you to miss out. God knows I've set this all up for your benefit."

"What are we doing out here?" Rowan asked meekly, a question he didn't want an answer to.

Sawyer jutted his chin toward the bank to their right, his hand still on Cody's neck. "See that boat over there? The little wooden thing? I figured we'd all climb aboard and set sail. See what's biting."

Rowan pulled his eyes over to where Sawyer was looking and saw a small, pathetic-looking craft that appeared mostly rotten. Calling it a boat was a stretch, but it appeared intact. It was an ancient thing though, as if someone had pulled it up onto the shore and then left it there a decade ago.

"Can we please go home...?" Rowan begged one last time, his voice quivering. The chain around Cody's neck clinked gently as the boy shivered in the night, sniffling weakly.

Sawyer raised the tire iron and leaned into Rowan, his voice hostile. "Not until we teach this animal that he can't mess with us. Now I'm going to start, but you're going to help me or so help me *god*, Rowan..."

The alarms in Rowan's head began to blare once again, louder than ever. Start? Start what? What exactly were they doing out here?

But before he could ask, Sawyer suddenly turned on Cody and raised the tire iron. Cody saw it coming and tried to shrink away, but Sawyer was too fast, his aim horribly accurate.

Cody's left knee took the brunt of the blow, shattering in an instant as the tire iron exploded down across it with all the force of hell behind it. Cody's mouth opened like some kind of terrible maw, a soundless expression of absolute agony, his eyes bulging from their sockets. He collapsed to the ground, his leg jutting out at an unnatural angle.

Sawyer immediately shifted so that he was standing over him, his eyes wild with hate, the iron rising over his head once more. When he brought it down a second time, across Cody's other knee, that was when the naked boy began to shriek. It was the sound of a wild animal who knew it was dying and could do nothing to stop it.

Without pause, Sawyer, teeth bared, slammed the tire iron down two, three, four more times across Cody's thighs and shins, shattering the bone so completely that the skin split apart and the shards could be seen jutting from the impact.

Rowan felt his legs give out and he landed on his backside with a thud, shock rolling through him as the barrage of violence continued in front of him. He had never seen anything so brutal in his entire life and he screamed internally for it to stop, to end, to please let it be over.

But it didn't end. Cody continued to scream as Sawyer beat his lower half into broken shards, the damage unmeasurable. Rowan watched, paralyzed, as Sawyer seemed to transform into something else, a wild dog with a thirst for pain and suffering.

Cody was on his stomach now, shrieking and trying to claw himself across the ground, blood oozing from his shattered legs. Sawyer saw this and tossed the iron aside, dropping to his knees to sit on the boy's back. He reached down and jerked Cody's head up by the hair, bending him backwards, paralyzing him in place.

And then, snarling, Sawyer opened his mouth and brought his teeth down into the boy's exposed back.

Rowan covered his face with his arms, curling up on the ground. He felt himself begin to cry as Cody's howls pierced his ears. He didn't know human beings could create sounds like the ones he was hearing and every ounce of him begged for it to end, please God, just let it end.

He didn't know how long it was before Sawyer stopped biting Cody, but it felt like hours. When Sawyer finally stood up, wiping blood from his lips, Cody had gone silent. Rowan slowly pulled his tear-soaked face out of his arms and looked across the bank at where the naked boy lay.

When he saw the state Cody was in, he tilted his head to the side and threw up, his stomach heaving in protest.

Sawyer stared down at Cody, panting. His eyes were large and wide as he surveyed the damage he had done.

"Fuck," he whispered hoarsely. "Fuck, fuck, fuck, I think I killed him." Sawyer dropped to his knees, like he was coming out of some kind of coma, and reached to check the boy's pulse. After a moment, he smiled, but it was a hollow thing.

"Thank god," He whispered. "The little bitch is still breathing. Jesus." He looked across at Rowan, that grotesque smile still plastered across his face. "Got a little carried away there, didn't I? Shit. You ever get like that? When your blood just boils over and you feel yourself falling into it?" He blinked. "Not a damn thing you can do to stop it either. It'd be like trying to stop a bullet with your head." Sawyer seemed to realize the state of distress Rowan was in and he climbed to his feet. "Hey you OK? Did you puke? Come on, man, I know I got a little worked up there, but you gotta have some balls. Don't you remember who this dirt stain is? What he did to you and Brenda?"

Rowan stayed on the ground and shut his eyes, his face wet, the ground around his head soaked in vomit. He didn't want to see, didn't want to breathe, didn't want to live another moment in this hell.

It has to end...it has to end...

Sawyer bent down and hauled Rowan to his feet. "Up you go. I told you you're going to help me finish this and I meant it. We're not done here."

Rowan felt dizziness hit him like a fist and he almost fell back down. When he looked at Cody again, at the dozens of angry, bleeding bite marks that covered his body, he dry-heaved, his heart drumming in a panic.

"Stop that," Sawyer said, annoyed. "Go push the boat into the water. I'm going to haul this sack of garbage over there."

Rowan didn't move, his mouth tasting of rot. He felt as if the earth would open its mouth and swallow him up and he pleaded for it to do so.

Sawyer smacked Rowan on the back of the head hard. "Move or I'll get hungry for dessert. Is that what you want?"

Rowan jerked himself into motion, his head feeling as if he had been clubbed with the world's largest hammer. Everything blinked and swam in and out of focus, the world tilted at a horrible angle, sloping him down into hell.

Sawyer picked up Cody's unmoving body and dragged him behind Rowan, towards the boat, the chain dragging in the dirt. Grunting, just wanting everything to end, Rowan pushed the small craft into the water, the hull scraping loudly against the rocks. When it was afloat, Sawyer splashed over to it and dropped Cody inside before hauling himself in as well. Before Rowan could protest, Sawyer grabbed him by the arm and jerked him up and into the rickety craft, spilling him across the opposite end. A single oar lay on the floor and Sawyer picked it up and tossed it to Rowan.

"Paddle us out. Hurry up."

Sniffling, with snot running down his face, Rowan dipped the oar into the water and began to slowly pull them across the surface of the pond. His muscles felt like liquid and every stroke of the oar drained him of energy he didn't possess. Sawyer watched him, holding the end of Cody's chain with one hand while the other rested on the side of the boat.

The moon illuminated the dark water, the tiny ripples reflecting its constant glow. As they neared the center of the pond, Rowan noted that dawn couldn't be far away, based on how low the moon had dipped in the sky.

"You shouldn't hate me for this," Sawyer said quietly, his face masked in shadow. "People like this, these kids, they're bad for the world. Think about it. What good could these two possibly do if they were allowed to grow up? You really think they'd change? Mature into decent folk?" Sawyer grunted. "That's just not how the world works. Some people are just born bad. They stalk kids like you and punish them for being good people. And it's no better when they grow up. The damage they do just gets worse. That's why we're doing this, Rowan. 'Cause they deserve it and I'm sick of letting trash like this skate by without consequence."

Rowan continued to row them out, the small boat sliding through the water soundlessly. He tried not to look at Cody's body lying on the bottom of the boat, but it was nearly impossible. The state he was in looked beyond measure and he wondered how he was still alive.

"Talk to me, Row," Sawyer growled. "You'll just piss me off otherwise."

Rowan stopped paddling and he let the boat glide into the deep water. He looked at Sawyer and when he did, all he felt was terror.

"I know they're bad," Rowan choked out, casting a glance at Cody. "I know they've done some bad things. But this...what you did to them..."

"Was their punishment," Sawyer finished. "People have gotten weak." He spat over the side. "Fact is, I'm the only one standing up for what's right. You used to be able to do something when someone treated you like shit. These days though, if you stand up for yourself you're just as likely to get in trouble. If someone calls you a name, you gotta hit them or they'll just keep doing it. If someone punches you, then you gotta break their arm. If someone hurts a person you care about, then you gotta bury that bastard." Sawyer leaned forward, across the boat, his voice hoarse, almost desperate. "You have to *set things right*, Rowan. It's our job as men to do that. You, me, even your father. If something bad happens, then it's our responsibility to bend it back, even if we end up breaking it."

Rowan felt as if his body had turned to shards of ice. "This won't make things better."

Sawyer's eyes burrowed into Rowan's as if digging into his mind. "You're too young still. You don't know what it's like. You haven't been beaten down yet." Sawyer leaned forward again, his voice a focused hiss.

"Let me tell you something I ain't ever told anyone. When I was younger, about ten years ago, right before I met Gayle, I was seeing someone else. Her name was Mia. She was a sweet thing, nothing but sunshine and cherry pie. We were together for some time. Years. Everything was good, great even, and I was actually happy. I started seeing things a little different, like the world had taken on a new coat of paint." Sawyer paused and his voice dropped to a hateful whisper.

"But then she got pregnant."

Rowan swallowed hard and looked away, the moon glistening off the water.

Sawyer continued, his voice burning in his throat. "At that point in time, I knew I couldn't have kids. It was impossible for me. But she didn't know that. I never told her. Didn't want to. I was embarrassed and ashamed, like somehow that made me less of a man. And so when she told me she had a bun in the oven, I didn't say anything. I was in shock. Absolute shock. I couldn't believe what she had done behind my back. I had been with some awful women, but she was different. She *had* to be different."

Sawyer ran his teeth over his bottom lip, his face twisted in a snarl. "In that moment, I just kept my mouth shut and waited for her to come clean. To show some hint of her betrayal. To show just an ounce of guilt. You know what she did though? She lied to my face. She played stupid. She acted like the kid was my doing, even though that wasn't possible. She told me she wanted to have it and said I'd make a great father, all the while completely oblivious to the fact that I knew she was full of shit. Hell, I even think I knew whose kid it really was, but I couldn't prove nothing."

"Sawyer—" Rowan pleaded.

"Shut up," Sawyer growled. "Just shut up and listen. You see, I kept waiting for her to come clean. To say something. To own up to what she did. I kept my mouth shut for weeks, burning up inside, dying each day she continued to lie to me. And you know what? She held her tongue until the very end. Until I was a husk. Until the bags under my eyes grew dark. Until I couldn't take the pain of her betrayal anymore. Until I couldn't stand to look at her without seeing something else. I forced the truth out of her. Me. She was six months pregnant. Six goddamn months she lied to me and tried to fill my head with a story that fit her vision."

Sawyer leaned back in the boat, his eyes gleaming with hatred. "All my life shit like that has happened to me with no consequence. I should have held her accountable. I should have made things right. But instead I just walked away, absolutely on fire with pain, and all she had to do was wave away the smoke before it stung her eyes and I was gone. You don't get to hurt a person like that and then force them to live in the toxic fallout of your own atomic nightmare. It's taken me a long fuckin' time to get to where I am now and I'm telling you kid, it's where I need to be. So when you say it won't make things better, you're dead wrong. Mental warfare deserves the same judgment as physical violence. And I'm making sure the two ends connect. You got that?"

Rowan let his eyes fall away, his voice choked behind his swollen throat. He knew it was useless to try to reason with Sawyer. Something had snapped in him and he had reached a point of no return. It was clear that he carried years of scars and nothing he could say or do would cover them up.

You just have to get out of this alive. Do whatever you have to or you'll be the one lying in the bottom of the boat.

Sawyer stood, rocking the boat some, and cleared his throat as if snapping out of some hateful trance. "This is far enough. Keep us steady, I'm going to wake him up." He wrapped the chain around his fist and then leaned down and slapped Cody a few times.

"Rise and shine, pal. We've reached the end of the road and it's time for you to get out."

Cody's head rolled to the side as Sawyer struck him, but after a moment, to Rowan's dismay, he opened his eyes, coughing. He blinked in the darkness, as if unsure where he was, but then the pain of his injuries hit him and he moaned loudly, his body shuddering.

"Knew you were a tough cookie," Sawyer said, reaching down to grab him by the hair. "I wouldn't want you to miss your send-off."

Cody's lips trembled as he was jerked up into a sitting position, his eyes finding Rowan's.

"Stop him," Cody begged weakly, tears leaking from his eyes. "Please don't let him kill me…"

Sawyer shook him roughly. "Shut the fuck up. You don't get to talk to him after what you've done."

And then he began to wrap the chain around Cody's body. He looped it first around his throat and then down the length of his naked, bleeding torso. When Cody saw what he was doing, he began to weep quietly, the fight beaten from him so completely that all he could do was sit and cry.

Rowan watched, feeling his heart swell. Tears reached his own eyes and he silently began to cry, a desperate, hopeless release that overwhelmed every ounce of him.

"I'm sorry," Rowan whispered, chest hitching. "I'm sorry, Cody."

Sawyer snapped his head up. "Stop that. Don't apologize to this waste of breath. He doesn't deserve it." He finished wrapping Cody in the chain and then hoisted him to the side of the boat. Cody was shaking so hard that the iron links clinked together. His face was consumed by terror as he stared down into the inky waters.

Sawyer leaned forward, his voice a whisper in Cody's ear. "If you hold your breath long enough, maybe you'll find forgiveness somewhere down there."

And then he shoved him overboard. There was a small splash, and then Cody was gone. Rowan felt a scream rise in his throat, but he didn't have the energy to release it. His eyes bulged as he stared at the expanding ripples, his heart crawling up his throat. He prayed that somehow Cody would break free, swim away, emerge on the opposite shore in a whooping gasp, hurt but safe.

But the surface of the water continued to smooth its edges and Cody did not surface.

He's gone.

Sawyer exhaled, an exhausted, satisfied expression. He sat back down in the boat and ran his hands over his face. When he spoke, his voice was grim and full of hatred.

"Get us back to land, Rowan. Our night isn't finished."

CHAPTER 12

Rowan stumbled out of the boat and hauled himself onto the shore. The moon continued to dip at his back, the sky now tinged with the faintest of grays. His feet squished across the muddy bank as Sawyer hauled the small craft onto the grass. When it was secure, he motioned for Rowan to follow him back toward the truck.

Rowan cast one last look over his shoulder at the calm waters and felt as if his soul had drowned down there as well. He was absolutely exhausted, drained, and broken, his mind a muddled mess of anguish, grief, and guilt. He wanted nothing more than to disappear forever, leaving nothing but a blank shadow in his wake. He couldn't believe how terrible the night had grown, how violent and bloody the man before him had become.

You need to run, he thought to himself as he trudged up the bank behind Sawyer. *You need to get away from him. He's still got that look on his face. There's more coming. You have to get away. Doesn't matter where.*

They walked around the cabin, headed toward the truck, each step closing his window of opportunity. He knew he had to go, but the fear of what he had just witnessed caused him to falter. What if he tried and Sawyer caught him? What then? Would he be the next victim? Would he be the tire iron's next meal?

It doesn't matter. You have to try. Do you really think you're going to walk away from this? Do you think he'll let you? He's not the man you thought he was. Not even close. Run, Rowan, run.

Almost to the truck now. Sawyer hadn't even turned around to see if he was following him. He seemed to have something else on his mind, as if Rowan were just a passing thought, a sidekick to his rampage.

Go. GO! Get help! Get away from him! GO ROWAN!

Rowan bolted for the woods, the last echo of his mind forcing him into action, breaking his terrified paralysis. Despite his exhaustion, he found that he practically flew past the cabin, headed directly for the treeline opposite the road. It was as if a bomb had gone off in his limbs, the fallout roaring through his chest. He didn't look behind him, didn't even breathe, he simply sprinted, his feet gliding like the wind.

He made it further than he could have possibly hoped for before Sawyer's voice called out to him, a surprised, angry eruption.

"Hey! HEY! Rowan get back here!"

Rowan burst through the treeline with a gasp, finally releasing the tightness in his chest. The hunt was on and he had a decent lead. The underbrush ripped at his clothes and the rocks beneath his feet tried their best to trip him up, but he kept moving. He bounced off trees, jumped over logs, the wind roaring in his ears, his pulse beating like a drum beneath his skull.

Don't stop. Don't ever stop.

Sawyer was coming. Rowan could hear his heavy footfalls beginning to thunder at his back, breaching the treeline in a crash of foliage.

Rowan had no idea where he was going, the dark of night blinding his path. His legs churned viciously, his hands held out in front of him like a shield. The forest blurred together like a bad nightmare, repeating itself over and over again, the stink of his own sweat burning his nose.

He's coming. He's getting closer.

"ROWAN GET THE FUCK BACK HERE!"

Rowan's throat seemed to close up, each gasp of air harder to swallow. His lungs began to roast over a coal fire and his legs began to slow. The woods continued to beat on him, each passing branch or rock crunching or clawing at his body, draining him of the precious energy he still possessed. Tears began to form in his eyes, not out of fear, but out of desperation.

"ROWAN!"

The crash of Sawyer's pursuit continued to grow louder, the older man's long legs pulling him toward his prey with every leaping step. Rowan knew this and yet he couldn't, wouldn't stop. The desperation began to give way to fear and soon his tears blinded him worse than the night.

With a whooping gasp, he suddenly tripped on something and went sprawling. His chin bounced off the woodland floor and he bit his tongue hard enough to draw blood.

Get up get up get up get—

Crying now, Rowan scrambled to stand, his legs and arms fighting him every step of the way. He was spent, could feel how drained he was, and yet he tried to get going again, his mouth pulled open in a frustrated, terrified expression of panic and fatigue.

Right as he got to his feet, something crashed into him hard enough to knock the wind from his lungs. He flew back down with a cry, crunching into the earth with a meaty thud as something heavy pressed down on top of him, pinning him in place.

Rough hands clawed at Rowan's neck and Rowan began to scream, the scent of alcoholic breath blasting over him.

"Got you," Sawyer snarled, his body pressing Rowan's to the ground. "Got you, got you, I fucking got you."

Rowan squealed and writhed in the dirt as Sawyer grabbed a handful of his hair and then slammed his face down into the ground hard enough to bring stars. Rowan let out an *oomph!* and his body went limp, darkness swarming the edges of his vision, giving clarity to the stars dancing before his eyes.

"You little rat," Sawyer hissed into his ear, his sweaty cheek pressed to Rowan's. "You ungrateful little rat. Where are you trying to scurry away to? Huh? You tryin' to leave me?"

"Sawyer, please—" Rowan heaved, crying, squirming.

But his plea was cut short as Sawyer pulled his shirt down, hard enough to rip it, exposing Rowan's bare shoulder.

"No! Sawyer I—" Rowan screamed, but his words turned to howls a second later as Sawyer buried his teeth into Rowan's flesh.

Rowan's feet drummed horribly against the ground, his body arching in shock, his eyes bulging. All thought evaporated and was replaced by a blinding white anchor of pain that dragged him to the edge of agony.

He could feel Sawyer's teeth digging into his shoulder, working the flesh loose. He could feel the blood pouring over his neck. He could feel the weight of his attacker pressing him into the dirt.

Rowan's eyes rolled in their sockets and he shrieked, the pain peaking as Sawyer tore away a chunk of him, his mouth filled with Rowan's bloody flesh.

Sawyer sat up and spit the gore away, his chin and teeth stained red. He wiped his mouth with a grimace.

"You're with me, Rowan," he said, his voice wet. "We're in this together all the way to the end."

Rowan's shrieks fell into gasping sobs as the pain in his shoulder ebbed and flowed, like fire in the wind. He could feel the night air lapping at the exposed muscle, at the hole in his shoulder that vomited blood onto his back. It felt like someone had dropped a burning rock onto him and was holding it in place.

"Can't believe you'd try to leave me," Sawyer continued, still sitting on Rowan, keeping him pinned. "After everything we've been through. You're just like everyone else. A complete and total fucking disappointment." He leaned forward, down into Rowan's sobbing face. "You broke my heart, kid. Broke it clean in two. Now I gotta set things right."

Before he could respond, Sawyer grabbed Rowan's left arm and yanked it behind his back. Rowan's eyes went wide as he suddenly felt an immense pressure building in his elbow. He opened his mouth to scream, knowing what was coming.

Sawyer broke the bone in one horrible, violent motion. Rowan heard it snap and then his body erupted in pain so severe he barely

heard himself howl. It sounded like some distant animal getting muti-
lated. It sounded completely inhuman.

Still screaming, Rowan's vision shuddered and then he blacked out.

In the darkness, he dreamed of an ocean. The water was the color
of ink and the sky was an overcast blanket that stretched across an
endless horizon. He was sinking—sinking deeper and deeper into
that terrible ebony abyss. Something was down there waiting for him.
Something huge and violent, its mouth agape. There was nothing he
could do to stop it. He couldn't slow, couldn't scream, couldn't escape.
He could sense it, lying across the ocean floor beneath his feet. He was
getting closer...closer...

Rowan opened his eyes and the world rushed back. The dream
lingered like a mist around his mind, but soon it began to burn away
as his senses returned.

Pain. That was the first thing he noticed. Burning, biting pain that
clung to his shoulder. He shifted hazily and let out a cry of agony
when he moved his left arm.

He broke your arm.

The thought acted like a wick, burning down into his chest to
explode, bringing everything back. Rowan blinked, exhausted, and sat
up, the world bouncing and bumping around him. The side of his head
struck something hard, bringing focus with it.

They were back in the truck. Sawyer was driving them somewhere,
his face edged with hard lines and fury. His eyes were glued to the
road, like a pair of dark wells that held nothing but darkness in their
depths. The pistol sat in his lap, ready to use at a moment's notice.

Groaning, whimpering, Rowan sat up across from him, resting his
face against the window, trying his best to temper the constant pain
that shot through his broken arm and burning shoulder.

Sawyer glanced at him, his voice like concrete falling on gravel.
"The more you move, the more it's going to hurt. Once we've finished
our business I'll patch you up. Get you in a splint. I'll keep an eye on it
as it heals, make sure it grows back right."

Rowan stared out the window, letting Sawyer's words wash over
him. He recycled what he had just been told, his mind still cold.

I'll make sure it grows back right.

How long will that take?

How long is he going to keep me?

How long until this is over?

And then.

This is the rest of your life.

Rowan closed his eyes and felt the tears come once more. They rolled silently down his face and stuck to the window. His cheek mashed against them, destroying the evidence of his grief. When he opened his eyes again, he pushed them past the window and out into the world.

We're out of the woods. Back on the main road. Are we going home? Back to the trailer park?

The sky had continued to brighten, the first flush of purple now blossoming over the gloomy foothills, extending out into the grassy fields. Morning birds had begun their song, chirping cheerfully as the truck roared by. To Rowan, it was the most depressing sound he had ever heard.

They don't know what's happened.

It's not their fault.

Let them sing while they can.

"You still with me, Row?"

Rowan pushed his head off the window and stared at Sawyer. His face felt puffy from all the crying, filthy from all the fighting.

"You're going to kill her, aren't you?" Rowan rasped.

Sawyer returned to the road. "She turned her back on me, kid. She's got to answer for that. You don't marry a man only to turn traitor. She snitched to your mother and she might have snitched to the cops. I've been patient with her, god knows I have, but it's time for Gayle to own up to what she's done."

Rowan turned back to the road, his pulse like sludge as a small yellow car passed them on the opposite side of the road. He wondered what the driver would think if they knew who they had just blown by.

"Why don't you kill me too then?" Rowan asked after a moment.

Sawyer jerked his head back, like he had been struck. "Kill you? Why would I do that?"

"You think I've turned on you, too. You said so back there."

Sawyer gripped the wheel, the road humming beneath them. "I haven't given up on you yet. I've seen the kind of kid you are, Row. I've seen your heart. There's hope for you yet. I just gotta show you the way. Until then, I'll stick with you. We're in this together now."

In this together...

Rowan leaned down into the footwell and vomited. It came out in chunks and dribbled down his legs. His mouth burned with the acid and he wiped his chin, eyes watering.

"Aw hell, kid," Sawyer mumbled, reaching across to open the glove compartment. He took out a handful of napkins and pressed them onto Rowan's lap. "Here, clean yourself up. You look like last week's leftovers."

With the glovebox still open, Sawyer spotted a silver package and retrieved it, his eyes lighting up.

"Hey, Rowan, you want a Pop-Tart? Might make you feel better."

Rowan pulled his head back and stared blankly out the window. He felt like he might puke again if he opened his mouth.

Sawyer shrugged and tore open the package. He ate the Pop-Tarts quickly, hungrily, like he hadn't eaten in years. When he was finished, he wiped his mouth with the back of his hand and tossed the wrapper down into the vomit.

"You're going to have to clean that up later," Sawyer said. "But first we have to handle our business. Just stick with me."

The red Ford bounced aggressively as they pulled off the main road and Rowan dragged his eyes back past the window. They had reached the trailer park. The tiny homes remained dark and silent as they passed by, the early hour locking the residents to their beds and dreams. Rowan silently begged for someone to come outside with a shotgun and shoot them both. Splatter their skulls across the gravel road and be done with it.

Nothing good was going to happen once the truck stopped.

As they approached Sawyer's trailer, the small home slowly coming into view around the bend, Rowan could physically feel Sawyer's demeanor change. It was like someone had shoved an iron rod up his spine and then sent electricity coursing through it.

"Looks like your parents are still asleep," Sawyer noted as he pulled the truck in. "That's good. We don't want to wake them. In and out. This shouldn't take long. Don't want to wake the neighbors."

He parked the truck in front of his trailer and Rowan stared longingly at his bedroom window only a couple dozen yards away. It suddenly seemed like the safest place in the world and his heart ached for it.

Sawyer stared at Rowan, as if sensing his yearning. "Don't go getting any funny ideas here. If you start shouting for help or something stupid, then I'm going to put this thing to use." He waved the gun. "Your mom seems like a nice lady. It'd be a shame if she weren't anymore."

Rowan felt fresh tears roll down his face, his eyes cemented to his trailer. His home. Internally, he began to scream for his parents to wake up. He prayed for it with all his might.

Come get me, Dad. I'm sorry for everything and I need you right now. Please. Wake up. Wake up and help me.

But Rowan's trailer remained dark.

Sawyer opened his door. "Get out. You're coming inside with me. And be quiet. Looks like Gayle's decided to sleep in as well. Bet she's sawing logs, as peaceful as can be now that I'm not there. She always did complain about my snoring. Ungrateful, miserable whore. Never knew what she had." Sawyer gripped the gun. "Well let's go in and show her, huh?"

Sawyer came around the outside of the truck and opened Rowan's door for him. When Rowan didn't move, Sawyer grabbed him impatiently and hauled him toward the trailer, toward Gayle, toward the end. Pain burst to life like fireworks across Rowan's body as he limped along, dragged by his collar, but he clamped his teeth shut to stifle a cry. He couldn't, wouldn't drag his mother into this. He wouldn't, couldn't expose her to this monster.

Your mom seems like a nice lady...

Sawyer climbed the front steps of his trailer and tried the door. It was open. Grinning like the reaper, Sawyer pushed Rowan inside, the outside world disappearing at their backs as the latch clicked in place.

To Rowan, it sounded like a nail being hammered into a coffin. His heart galloped in his chest as he stumbled forward into the small living room, his elbow throbbing, his shoulder burning.

The inside of Sawyer's place was neat, with everything put away in its place. A small sofa rested against the wall, facing an old tube TV with a pair of bunny ears sprouting from the top. The kitchen counter to their right had been wiped down and a couple of empty cans had been left out for recycling. The air was still and silent, like the trailer itself was still asleep. An aroma wafted through the space, as if someone had lit incense the night before.

Sawyer scrubbed his nose with the back of his hand, the one holding the gun, as if repulsed by the smell.

"She always lit that shit after we had a fight," he growled, his eyes going to the small hallway. "Thought it'd clear the air of any anger between us. Guess she should've kept it burning a little longer. Come on, move Rowan, down the hall."

"Please don't do this," Rowan sputtered as he was shoved forward.

Sawyer ignored him, pushing them both across the matted carpet toward the closed door at the end of the hall. As they walked, Rowan could feel Sawyer tensing, like a predator preparing to pounce on his prey.

Please let her be gone, Rowan prayed as they approached the door. *Please God, don't let her be in that room.*

Sawyer released Rowan for a moment and wrapped his hand around the doorknob. Slowly, he pushed it open.

Rowan's heart sank and the life drained from his face.

Gayle lay asleep on the bed before them, as naked as the day she had been born. A sweaty sheet half-covered her thighs, pulled down to expose her bare back and drooping breasts. She stirred as the doorknob tapped the wall, swinging wide and coming to a stop. Her eyes fluttered, the noise disrupting her dreams.

Sawyer pushed Rowan into the room, panting, and together they approached the bed. Rowan tried not to look at Gayle's exposed breasts, repulsed by himself for doing so, but he couldn't stop himself.

It was the first time he had seen a woman naked and it shocked him, as if all the stories were true.

It also made him sick to his stomach, repulsed by his own unwillful draw to them. He slammed his eyes shut, hating himself as they came to a stop at the foot of the bed.

Sawyer reached down and squeezed Gayle's foot through the sheet, his voice like a warship breaking through a dam.

"Rise and shine, babe. Daddy's come home."

Gayle's eyes practically burst open, her foot jerking up the bed. Her reaction was so instant and severe that Rowan jumped, thumping into Sawyer. Gayle scrubbed her eyes, dazed, her hair damp and matted across her forehead. She released a noise from her throat that sounded like some kind of stunned question, a fragment of confusion that bubbled up from her chest in bits and pieces. When her eyes locked with Sawyers', her face went pale and some of the uncertainty drained away, only to be replaced by rising fear. It was a look that burned itself into Rowan's mind like a brand. It was a singular expression that told him everything he needed to know about how this was going to go.

We're going to die.

"You getting your eight hours in, sweetie?" Sawyer said sickly, placing a hand on Rowan's shoulder.

Gayle scurried up the length of the bed and pressed herself against the headboard, her eyes shuddering and huge, her mouth open in a permanent expression of shock.

"Close your mouth, Gayle," Sawyer instructed, his voice low. "You look like a cow when you do that."

Gayle clicked her teeth shut and brushed the damp hair off her forehead. She licked her lips nervously and tried again to express sound.

"I—I—I—I thought you left me," she managed to gasp, finally noticing Rowan. She reached for the sheet to cover herself.

Sawyer slowly lowered himself and sat on the edge of the bed, smiling. "I'd never leave you, baby." He brought the gun into view. "But is that what you want? Do you want me to leave?"

Gayle's face tightened and she clutched the sheet harder, her eyes glued to the gun. She cleared her throat and tested a smile. "Of course not! I was worried—"

"Shut the fuck up."

Sawyer's voice dropped like a hammerblow over Gayle and she froze, her eyes darting first to the gun, then Rowan, then back to Sawyer.

"My good buddy here tells me you've been running your mouth," Sawyer continued, nodding to Rowan. "Says you've been saying all kinds of things about me. He tells me you were thinking about running to the cops over some lost kid." Sawyer reached out, his hand like a weaving snake, and gripped Gayle's ankle. "Now tell me that ain't true, baby. Tell me you wouldn't break my heart like that."

Gayle tried to pull away from Sawyer's touch, but he held her tight as she fumbled for an explanation.

"I—I—I was just worried about you!" She hurried, pleaded. "I thought you were in trouble and I wanted to help you! Sawyer, honey, you know I love you, you know I'd never—"

Suddenly Sawyer yanked her hard, pulling at her ankle and jerking her down the bed toward him. She slid on her back with a yelp and then Sawyer had the gun in her mouth, staring down at her with a hand around her throat.

"Shut your fucking *cunt* mouth or I swear to god I'll put a bullet in you. I'll blast it all the way down your lying, snitchin' throat like a hot, thick load. Do you understand me?"

Gayle's eyes bulged in her head and she nodded, her lips wrapped around the short barrel. She was shaking, shaking so hard her teeth clicked against the metal.

Sawyer leaned down into her face. "Now why don't you get into the kitchen and make Rowan and I some goddamn breakfast?"

As Gayle was let up, Rowan, in a daze, saw that she had wet the bed.

CHAPTER 13

Sawyer and Rowan sat at the kitchen table, watching as Gayle stumbled around the small kitchen. She was crying. Her naked thighs were stained with piss and the smell mixed with the eggs she was frying. The combination filled Rowan's head with poison, dragging him deeper into the bog that drowned his mind. He sat slumped over next to Sawyer, his eyes twin pits of despair, his shoulders drooping, his face gaunt, hollow, and exhausted. Every breath he took brought in more poison. Every second that ticked by was another eruption inside his skull. He could feel himself needing to cry, but the thought of it, the effort needed, was so far beyond him that it remained a distant mirage.

"You like eggs?" Sawyer grunted.

Rowan's mouth remained slack, the question passing him by like a shadow at full dark.

"I don't like eggs," Sawyer continued, sitting upright in a kitchen chair, his legs splayed out before him, the gun resting on his crotch. "Don't know why this bitch is making us eggs. What's wrong with toasting a couple of Pop-Tarts?"

Sawyer sat up a little straighter. "Gayle, what the hell are you doing over there? How long have we been together? Don't you know I hate that shit? Where is your head at?"

Gayle froze in the tiny kitchen, her hands hovering over the sizzling frying pan, a trio of eggs popping merrily before her. She looked over her shoulder at Sawyer and Rowan, his eyes rimmed red.

"W—what?" she stuttered, her sobs staggered.

Sawyer stood up. "I asked you to perform a simple task. Make breakfast. That's it. It's not rocket science. What are you doing?"

Gayle looked at Sawyer and then frantically cast her eyes across the kitchen as if searching for some kind of clue, some way to stop Sawyer's rampage.

"What are you *doing*?" Sawyer repeated. He placed the gun down on the table and marched over to Gayle, towering over her. "You know I hate eggs. I've hated them my whole life. So I'll ask you again—what are you doing?"

Gayle jerked herself against the stove, knees shaking. "I—I—I'm sorry, I don't know what I was th—th—thinking. Of course you don't like e—e—eggs."

Sawyer stared down at her, his eyes dark. "Are you trying to get in one last jab? Is that it? Haven't you done enough? Don't you know how much trouble you're already in?"

"Sawyer I—"

"Shut up," Sawyer hissed. "Just shut up. I'm so *tired* of you." He turned, closed his eyes, and squeezed the bridge of his nose. "What do you think, Rowan? The hell am I supposed to do with her?"

Rowan stared at the gun on the table. It was all he could see. It was like a glistening body of water in the middle of the desert.

It's right there.

"Why don't *you* eat the eggs, dear?" Sawyer said suddenly, popping his eyes back open. "I'm sure you're hungry. Are you hungry, sweetie?"

The world shimmered.

I could pick the gun up and end this right now.

But Sawyer was standing just a couple feet away.

And he's fast. I've seen how fast he can be.

Sawyer approached Gayle, one hand reaching for the sizzling pan of eggs. "Don't be ashamed, honey, everyone gets hungry. Let me show you what a good husband does for his wife. Let me feed you. Let me provide for you just like I always have, you ungrateful fucking hog."

With each word, Sawyer's voice rose, his fingers finding the frying pan, lifting it from the burner. Gayle backed away, hands raised, her mouth open in hope that some kind of plea would come bubbling out.

"That's right, open up bitch, here comes a couple of hot ones over easy." Sawyer growled, lunging forward to grab Gayle by the back of the neck.

Gayle shrieked and tried to shrink away, but Sawyer held her still. In one jarring, awful motion, he slammed the lip of the burning-hot pan into Gayle's mouth and held her in place as he tipped the sizzling eggs down into her face.

Gayle's howls filled the trailer as she shuddered and writhed, her skin burning and tearing away as it stuck and ripped across the hot surface. The three eggs landed across her face and ruptured, vomiting boiling-hot yellow across her eyes and down her cheeks.

Sawyer threw the pan down, his face red. "Eat up honey bunches cause this is going to be your last fucking meal! You hear me!? I'm fucking DONE with you."

Sawyer jerked the shrieking woman across the kitchen and then threw her into the burning stove. Gayle screamed and wept, blinded by the dribbling, steaming yolk as her hands collided with the still glowing elements. She stumbled backwards, crashing into the cabinets, clawing at her eyes, her throat bloated with pained screams, her veins swelling beneath her skin. She fell to the floor, completely lost in herself, and began to claw her way across the floor toward the living room.

Scowling, his face brimming with hatred, Sawyer stepped over her and booted the side of her face. "Don't you dare try to run from what you are, you hear me? You lay there and take it like the traitorous rat you are."

The gunshot that came next brought silence in the wake of its sudden, violent eruption. It arrived without announcement and froze the world in its place, filling the trailer with the smell of burning gun smoke.

Sawyer slowly, carefully, turned to face Rowan. When he spoke, his voice was low and careful.

"What on earth do you think you're doing, boy?"

Rowan held the gun on Sawyer, tears running silently down his face.

Sawyer raised his hands slowly, backing away from Gayle now. "Don't you point that thing at me, kid. I know you don't wanna pull that trigger again and god knows I don't want you to actually hit me this time so let's all just take a damn breath, OK?"

"Stop it…" Rowan choked, his mind rolling in a tide of grief, exhaustion, and confusion. "You have to stop it…"

Sawyer nodded. "OK, OK. Sure. I've stopped."

Rowan's chest hitched once, twice, the sobs surging on the waves across his ribs. "Just stop hurting her...please…"

Gayle moaned, her body shaking, and pulled herself over to the couch where she lay shivering, weeping, her face a pulpy yellow mess.

Sawyer gestured to her. "See, look, she's OK. I've stopped. That's what you wanted, right? Rowan? Talk to me. Put the gun down and talk to me. We're supposed to be friends."

"I'm not your friend," Rowan cried. "Not like this."

Sawyer's face suddenly changed. It went from caution to genuine confusion, and then the hurt came. It started in his eyes and then bled across his face.

"What?" was all he said before the front door exploded open, letting in the warm morning sunlight.

Rowan threw up a hand, momentarily blinded by the blast of light. In that moment, Sawyer sprang for him. He tackled Rowan into the kitchen table, knocking the gun out of his hand. Rowan felt the air leave his lungs and his broken arm ignited in agony as it bounced off a chair, sending shock waves coursing through his body. He landed heavily, dazed, and felt Sawyer land next to him, the gun lost.

"STOP THIS!"

The voice came from the open doorway, a bellowing command that Rowan recognized in an instant. He had grown up with that voice in his ear. In his head.

Dad…?

Rowan scrambled away from Sawyer, his arm aching like it had been dipped in acid. He rolled over and bumped into Gayle, who was whimpering on the floor, curled into a ball. When he gained his bearings a second later, he finally looked up.

George towered in the doorway, his figure ignited by the sun. He took one look at what was happening and then he threw himself at Sawyer, who was regaining his feet. The two men crashed into the table, breaking it, throwing splinters across the kitchen in an eruption of wood.

"What have you DONE!?" George roared as he wrestled with Sawyer, the pieces of violence all around him fitting together like some kind of terrible puzzle.

"Get off of me!" Sawyer yelled, finding his fist and throwing it into George's jaw. George winced and rolled away, scrambling to his feet, his face slick with sweat. As he stood up, panting, he looked to Rowan, his eyes wide.

"What happened here?" he gasped, the words trying to slot together the chaos around him. "Are you hurt?! Rowan!"

Rowan looked toward his father and felt himself begin to cry once more. He tried to speak, but everything died in his throat in a wash of misery.

"This isn't your business," Sawyer growled as he stood, squaring off with George. "This is between me and my wife."

George pointed to Rowan, his face red. "What have you done to him!? Where have you BEEN!?"

"Get out of my house," Sawyer snarled, circling him. "I'm only going to ask once."

George looked past Rowan at Gayle, and the wind whistled from his lungs. "God have mercy, what did you do to her?"

"Nothing she didn't have coming."

George looked back to Rowan, his hands curling into fists. "I need you to run, son. Your mother called the police once we heard the screaming. Get to her."

"You called the cops?" Sawyer spat, disgust and rage rolling across his face like a summer storm. "You ratted me out!? I thought we were neighbors. I thought we were *men*."

"You're an animal," George rumbled. "A wild *dog*."

Sawyer flew into George with all the force he could muster. His shoulder connected with George's chest, and the two men crashed into the wall by the door. George let out an awful, pained noise and slumped into Sawyer, his hands reaching for his attacker's throat. Sawyer swatted them away and then leaned in.

His teeth came down over George's neck and then he bit. He bit hard, the splash of blood instant, the tear of flesh like the rip of fabric. George cried out in pain and then he brought his forehead crunching down into Sawyer's face. The two men collapsed as one, fists flying, jaws snapping, desperate to gain the upper hand over the other.

Rowan's heart was racing, each beat like thunder inside his head. He watched the two men, his own father, fighting for their lives, every second pulling closer to an imminent death. A hand touched his arm and he almost screamed as the tornado of violence continued to rage before him. He looked down and saw Gayle pointing beneath the shattered table, her one good eye poking out from beneath a swamp of yellow.

"Gun," was all she said.

Rowan whipped his head around and spotted the small pistol beneath the debris. Gasping, he crawled for it, his muscles igniting once more, his arm howling in protest. Behind him, Sawyer had rolled on top of George and had begun to rain down blows, each punch connecting with a wet, meaty weight. George threw his hands up, trying to protect his face, but each time he did, Sawyer went for the ribs, pummeling them like a man gone mad.

Gasping, crying, Rowan reached the gun. His fingers curled around the grip and the familiar weight returned as he lifted it.

Sawyer, unaware, continued to beat George, his mouth contorted in rage, his voice a venomous hiss.

"You don't get to come in here and tell me what to do," he panted as he landed another blow. "You're not God in this house."

"SAWYER!"

Sawyer's head snapped up as Rowan's voice exploded over the vicious beating, freezing everything for a moment. When Sawyer saw the gun pointed at him, the blood drained from his face.

"Hey whoa," he said quickly, the fight frozen in his veins. "Hey come on kid let's—"

"*Stop,*" Rowan whimpered.

He pulled the trigger. The gun bucked in his hand, but the bullet flew true. It plowed into Sawyer's shoulder and tore him off George in an eruption of blood. Sawyer grunted and spun with the impact, slamming his head into the wall, dazing him.

Rowan dropped the gun, hands shaking, the world spinning.

I shot him shot him shot him shot him—

Everything was buzzing and ringing and burning and aching and—

George crawled to his feet, his face bloodied. Sawyer twisted on the ground, teeth clenched, mouth working soundlessly. He pressed a hand to his wound, trying in vain to stem the flow of blood.

George loomed over him, panting, blood dripping from his split nose and down his injured neck.

"You hurt my son."

Sawyer struggled to sit against the wall, feet kicking. Pain was plastered across his face, but he still held hate in his eyes like it was a life force.

"Your son had it coming. Everyone has to pay their dues," Sawyer growled as more blood spurted from between his fingers.

"You nearly killed your wife," George hissed, his hands curled like claws. "What kind of man does that?"

"What do you know about being a man?" Sawyer spat. "Your son is here because he hates you."

"My son is everything to me," George whispered so fiercely it was almost lost. "And you've nearly ruined him."

Before Sawyer could protest, George raised a booted foot and brought it crunching down into Sawyer's face. The impact bounced Sawyer's head across the floor, and blood exploded from the contact.

George raised his foot again and the second blow sent teeth flying across the floor.

The third one killed Sawyer. The force of the connection crunched through bone. His body ceased to move in an instant and his cries turned to empty air.

Rowan watched all of this from another world, one veiled behind a curtain of disbelief, horror, and most sickening of all, gratitude. He saw his father pull his foot from the cavity of Sawyer's face and wipe it on the floor. He saw the blood pooling. He could hear someone speaking to him, but it was a language he couldn't quite understand.

George limped to Rowan and knelt down, wiping blood from his nose. He was breathing heavily. His eyes were burning. He took Rowan's hands in his own and stared down into his son's face.

"It's over," he said gently. "It's over, Rowan." George seemed to slump with exhaustion. "My *god*."

Rowan blinked and looked up into his dad's face, almost unrecognizable to him. He could hear Gayle pulling herself up onto the couch next to him, sobbing and thanking George for saving them.

But George didn't look at her. Not yet. He pulled Rowan close and ran a hand over his son's head.

His voice was gentle. Soft. "I'm so *sorry*."

Rowan came out from behind the veil, the world shuddering in on him. His mind folded and he began to weep. He leaned into his father's chest and felt his father's arms encompass him, cradle him.

"Thank you," Rowan sobbed. "Thank you, thank you, *thank you*, Dad. Oh god...Dad...I didn't mean for this—"

Suddenly Rowan felt something wet drip down onto his head and when George spoke again, Rowan realized that he was crying softly.

"Hush now." George pulled Rowan closer to him, his breath stuttered and pained. "You don't have to say anything. This ain't your fault. Whatever this is, it ain't your fault, son."

The open doorway darkened once more and then Rose appeared, stumbling into the bloody trailer with wide eyes and an open mouth.

"What on earth—" she spotted Sawyer, dead on the floor, and shoved a fist into her mouth, stifling a scream.

"Are the police coming?" George croaked, turning his head toward his wife. "Did you call them?"

Rose nodded slowly, absorbing the scene before her with wide-eyed horror. She spotted Rowan in George's arms and she flew to him.

"Oh baby, what happened?! Oh God, what did he do to you!?"

"There will be time for that later," George whispered, not letting go of Rowan. "He's OK though. He's alright, Rose. He's alive."

Rose cupped her son's face in her hands, her eyes massive and full of worry. "Tell me you're OK, Row. Please. Please, whatever happened here, just tell me you're OK."

Rowan couldn't bear his mother's look, her concerned, loving eyes. It was overwhelming and the shame of what he had taken part in collapsed in on him like the walls of a cavern. He sunk deeper into his father's arms and cried silently, his shoulders shaking weakly.

Rose sat back on her heels, mouth opening and closing wordlessly as she tried to piece together what had transpired. She looked up at Gayle who was huddled on the couch, as if seeing her for the first time.

"Holy Christ," Rose shuddered, quickly standing. She rushed to the battered woman. "Oh sweetie, what did he do to you?"

Rowan didn't hear the rest. His whole world rumbled as his father spoke to him quietly, leaning down into his face, his eyes wet.

"Listen to me Rowan," he said gravely, his voice shaking behind a fragile emotional barrier. "The police are going to be here soon and things are going to get very complicated. I need you to do exactly as I say, do you understand?"

Rowan nodded slowly, tears streaming down his face. His eyes moved past his father and over toward Sawyer's ruined corpse.

Oh my god what did I do—

George shook him gently. "Don't look at him. Listen to me. I shot him. Do you understand? You had nothing to do with this. He was hurting you and Gayle and I wrestled the gun from him. I did this. All of this."

Rowan's eyes went wide, filling with tears, his mouth opening. "No, Dad, you don't—"

"Hush," George croaked, desperate now, his own face threatening to break like a dam. "You didn't shoot him. I did. And then I...I finished it. Say it back to me. Say it back to me, Row."

Rowan folded into himself, his arm throbbing. "Dad..."

"Please," George begged, the word rattling up his throat. "Please, Row. This is what I'm supposed to do. This is what I've *failed* to do." George looked away, tears forming in his eyes. "I'm supposed to *protect* you from people like him." He hurriedly wiped his eyes as the sounds of sirens began to fill the distance. "Now say it."

"I...I didn't shoot him," Rowan whispered miserably, his vision blurry.

George pressed Rowan's head gently to his chest, his hands running over his son's face. "Good boy." And then, a whisper. "I'll make this right."

CHAPTER 14

Rowan slowly opened his eyes. The familiar chirp and buzz of the hospital filled his head as the world began to come into focus, aligning itself in a blend of color and sound. The steady beep of the heart rate monitors. The slightly sour, sterile smell of the room he was in. The distant chatter of low voices.

Rowan shifted in his bed, awkwardly adjusting his cast in his sling. He didn't even remember getting it. After the horror in Sawyer's trailer, the following hours had become a wash of exhausted memory. He closed his eyes, sensing his mother close by, and tried to center himself. His chest felt tight, and the wound on his back where Sawyer had bit him burned beneath its bandage.

So much happened.

The cops had come, just as George had said. They had entered the scene and George had given himself up without a struggle. Rowan had been separated from his mother and father, hurried to a police car where they waited on an ambulance. They had prodded him with gentle questions, but Rowan had just stared at the ground, his eyes red-rimmed, his mind empty and shell-shocked. At one point, after the ambulance and paramedics had arrived, he spotted his father being handcuffed and shoved into the back of a police car. It was a terrifying scene, the one he had feared most, but his mother had arrived at his side shortly after and tried to console him, asking tearful questions in the process.

Rowan had stayed silent and at some point during their rush to the hospital, he had begun to cry again in his mother's arms. At that point, Rose just held him and wept silently along with her son.

Nothing made sense. From the very beginning.

Rowan heard someone speak his name, intruding into his thoughts.

How could this have happened?

"Rowan?"

Cody...Travis...

"Row?"

A hand on his leg, fingers brushing over the sheets. Rowan looked up and saw his mother, her frame perched in a chair beside his bed, her figure backed by the dark windows of the hospital.

Night? How long have I been here? A day? Two?

"Can I get you anything? Anything at all?" Rose asked gently. Rowan stared at his mother and noted how bad she looked. Her skin was tight across her cheekbones and her lips were white. There was a wild look in her eyes that scared him.

I bet if you looked in a mirror you'd see the same thing.

Rowan turned away from his mother.

What else would I see?

"Sweetie, please. You have to talk to me."

Rowan stared out of the open door of his hospital room. He spotted doctors and nurses scurrying about, all looking panicked and rushed.

Do they have any idea what happened?

"Row?"

Rowan cleared his throat, his voice a crawling whisper. "Where's Dad?"

Rose paused for a moment. The large windows at her back seemed to fill with despair and press into the room.

"He's being questioned. He's still at the police station."

Rowan closed his eyes, a headache on the horizon. And something worse.

"How long have I been here?"

"Two days. There's a very nice woman who wants to talk to you, but only when you're feeling better."

Rowan snapped his eyes open. "Feeling better?" He rolled his head across the pillow and stared at his mother. "Do you have any idea what I did, Mom?"

Rose's face collapsed with concern and she leaned forward, her hands fussing with the sheets. "I don't. I don't have any idea, Row. But if you want to talk about it, you can. I won't be mad. None of this was your fault."

"*Everything* was my fault."

"Don't say that. Please."

"I'm not a good person," Rowan said quietly, his throat closing up.

"Of course you are," Rose pleaded. "I'm your mother and I know what kind of son I raised. Whatever Sawyer did to you isn't your fault. Sometimes bad people get their claws into you and all you can do is try to get away from them."

Rowan closed his eyes. "Go away, Mom. Please." His eyes began to moisten then. "*Please.*"

Rose struggled to keep herself under control as she nodded. "OK sweetie. OK. But there's someone outside who's been waiting a very long time to talk to you and she won't leave until she does. I think you should let her in."

"If it's that woman—"

"It's not," Rose said. "It's a friend. She wants to see you."

Rowan opened his eyes and turned toward the door. When he saw who it was, some of the pain melted away.

"Brenda?"

Brenda stood awkwardly in the doorway with her mother at her back. She raised a timid hand.

"Hi Rowan."

Rose stood up. "Is it OK if she stays in here with you for a little bit?"

Rowan nodded. "Yeah. OK."

Rose walked to the door and left the room, followed with a sad smile by Brenda's mother, leaving the two alone.

"Um, do you want to sit down?" Rowan asked.

Brenda smiled and shuffled over, plopping herself into Rose's chair. She scooted it closer and stared down at Rowan, her eyes worried.

"Does it hurt?" she asked after a moment, pointing to Rowan's arm.

"No. Not anymore."

"What happened to it?"

"Sawyer broke it."

Brenda swallowed hard and leaned back a little. "The man who saved us at the barbeque?"

"Yeah."

"Why did he break your arm?"

Rowan looked down at himself, his mind tumbling. "I don't know. I think he was disappointed in me. I think he was sick."

Brenda's voice dropped to almost a whisper. "Hey Rowan?"

"Yeah?"

Brenda's eyes filled with tears. "Are you OK?"

Rowan tried to smile, but found that he couldn't. He turned away from Brenda and fought to keep himself under control, but it was a useless battle.

No. No I'm not OK.

"Do you want me to lay with you for a little bit?"

Rowan wiped his eyes and nodded, scooching over in his bed. Brenda climbed in next to him and laid her head down on the pillow. He could smell her hair, that wonderful, slightly sweet aroma that he instantly recognized. He felt her reach for his good hand and he accepted it, his heart fluttering.

"I'm sorry he did bad things to you," Brenda said softly. "I never did say thank you for sticking up for me back in the bathroom during the barbeque. I thought about that a lot afterwards. You knew they were going to beat you up, but you didn't care. You went charging in at them anyway."

Rowan shrugged, trying to push all the noise out of his head and just enjoy the sensation of her hand in his.

She doesn't know what you've done.

"When word got round about what happened to you, I told my mom we had to come see you," Brenda continued. "I didn't know how bad you were hurt. I was scared you were going to die."

"I'm not going to die," Rowan whispered.

"Hey Rowan?"

"Yeah?"

"When you get better, do you want to go get some ice cream with me?"

Rowan turned his head and stared at her, their faces inches apart. She stared back, their eyes meeting and swimming together, a warmth emanating between them.

"I'd like that a lot," Rowan whispered. He felt his chest tighten and again he was threatened with an outbreak of sorrow, a sobbing, awful cry that lingered deep down inside.

Brenda smiled and squeezed Rowan's hand. "We don't have to talk anymore." And then she snuggled into him, her soft skin brushing against Rowan's, sending shivers up his spine, excited, hopeful sparks of a future beyond today.

Rowan pulled the covers up and closed his eyes against her cheek. Silence blossomed between them and the horror of the past few days seemed to lose some of its bite. It didn't vanish and Rowan knew it never would. But some of the shock, the terror that clung to him like a second skin, seemed to ebb away. If only for a little while.

Sawyer's gone, Rowan thought as his eyelids began to close, his exhaustion catching up with him once more.

He can't hurt me anymore. He can't hurt anyone.

And then, following close behind in the calming darkness…

I need to see Dad. I have to be there for him. I bet he's scared.

Almost asleep now.

I have to make things right.

THE END

ELIAS WITHEROW currently lives up in New England and can usually be found muttering to himself as he stares out a window. Having authored over sixty short stories and seven novels, he hopes to continue to provide entertaining horror fiction to his readers. Also, if you ever see him at a metal show, be sure to say hi. He'd love that.

TWITTER @ELIASWITHEROW
FACEBOOK.COM/FEEDTHEPIG
REDDIT.COM/R/FEEDTHEPIG

THOUGHT
CATALOG
Books

Thought Catalog Books is a publishing imprint of Thought Catalog, a digi-tal magazine for thoughtful storytelling. Thought Catalog is owned by The Thought & Expression Company, an independent media group based in Brooklyn, NY, which also owns and operates Shop Catalog, a curated shop-ping experience featuring our best-selling books and one-of-a-kind prod-ucts, and Collective World, a global creative community network. Founded in 2010, we are committed to helping people become better communicators and listeners to engender a more exciting, attentive, and imaginative world. As a publisher and media platform, we help creatives all over the world real-ize their artistic vision and share it in print and digital form with audiences across the globe.

ThoughtCatalog.com | Thoughtful Storytelling

ShopCatalog.com | Boutique Books + Curated Products

Collective.world | Creative Community Network